"I don't think that would be a good idea," Rory said

"What?"

"For you to kiss me."

"Excuse me?"

"You were thinking about kissing me, and I'm telling you it's not a good idea."

"No, I wasn't."

She was looking at him as though she knew otherwise.

That's *not* what he'd been thinking. Was it? Mitch was pretty sure he hadn't had a coherent thought since he'd walked in and found her asleep on the sofa, but damn it, now that she'd suggested it, kissing her was all he could think about.

Dear Reader,

San Francisco, with its many unique and diverse neighborhoods, is one of my favorite cities in the world. After my first visit, I knew I had to set at least one story there.

I was particularly intrigued to find a school—the William R. DeAvila Elementary School—just a few short blocks from the world-famous Haight-Ashbury intersection. I wondered what it would have been like to raise a family in that neighborhood "back in the day" and what it would have been like for children to grow up and attend school there. *Firefighter Daddy* is the answer to that question.

This elementary school has served several different purposes in recent years, including a satellite campus for a community college. I have taken the liberty of reinventing this neighborhood's public elementary school, which I haven't given a name, and I hope you will forgive me for that.

Single dad Mitch Donovan and confirmed bachelorette Rory (Miss Sunshine to her students) Borland have both returned to their childhood homes, for very different reasons, and their story is set around this school. I hope you enjoy reading it as much as I did writing it, and I'd love it if you'd drop by my Web site at www.leemckenzie.com, where you'll find lots of fun stuff, including instructions for playing hopscotch.

Happy reading!

Lee McKenzie

Firefighter Daddy

LEE MCKENZIE

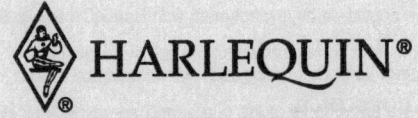

HARLEQUIN®

TORONTO • NEW YORK • LONDON
AMSTERDAM • PARIS • SYDNEY • HAMBURG
STOCKHOLM • ATHENS • TOKYO • MILAN • MADRID
PRAGUE • WARSAW • BUDAPEST • AUCKLAND

Recycling programs
for this product may
not exist in your area.

ISBN-13: 978-0-373-75320-8

FIREFIGHTER DADDY

ABOUT THE AUTHOR

From the time she was ten years old and read *Anne of Green Gables* and *Little Women*, Lee McKenzie knew she wanted to be a writer, just like Anne and Jo. In the intervening years she has written everything from advertising copy to an honors thesis in paleontology, but becoming a four-time Golden Heart finalist and a Harlequin Books author are among her proudest accomplishments. Lee and her artist/teacher husband live on an island along Canada's west coast, and she loves to spend time with two of her best friends—her grown-up children.

Books by Lee McKenzie

HARLEQUIN AMERICAN ROMANCE
1167—THE MAN FOR MAGGIE
1192—WITH THIS RING

I especially want to thank the dedicated firefighters
at the San Francisco Fire Department's Station 12
for welcoming me to their station and
patiently answering all my questions.
If this story contains inconsistencies with
traditional firefighting practices, I take
full responsibility for them and offer my apologies.

Chapter One

Mitch Donovan hadn't been inside this second-grade classroom since...well, second grade. He noticed two things right away—the chairs were a lot smaller than he remembered, and the teacher was much younger. He lowered himself into the chair next to his daughter's and tried to figure out what to do with his legs. He finally gave up and let them stretch into the middle of the circle, crossed at the ankles.

"Daddy?" Miranda whispered, gazing up at him.

"What?" he whispered back.

She produced a small square of folded paper from her pocket. "Miss Sunshine wants me to introduce you. She helped me write a speech and everything."

"That's great, honey." He caught the teacher's eye and wondered if he'd be reprimanded for talking in class. Not likely, given the boisterous behavior of two boys who were supposed to be clearing off their desks. There were days when being the parent of one seven-year-old was overwhelming, so he had a healthy respect for anyone who could spend all day with a room full of them.

He didn't know why the kids called her Miss Sunshine. Maybe because her clothing made him want to put on a pair of sunglasses. According to all the official school notices and the nameplate on the classroom door, her real name was Ms. Pennington-Borland. She was clearly of the era when parents hadn't batted an eye at bestowing awkward-sounding double-barreled names on their kids. So was he, but luckily his parents had stopped short of that.

He watched as she patiently guided a little girl who was printing something in a notebook, and then herded the last of the stragglers into the circle. She took the chair directly across from him and although she was significantly taller than all of the children, the chair accommodated her very nicely. Her bright flower-patterned skirt flowed demurely over her knees, exposing only a slender pair of ankles and dainty bare feet in white sandals.

"Children, we have a special visitor today. We've been learning about the different kinds of jobs people have, and Miranda's father is here to tell us about what he does. So before I ask her to introduce him, I want everyone to put on their best manners…"

With a series of grossly exaggerated motions, the children pretended to put their arms into some kind of invisible garment.

"…and our thinking caps so we can all ask lots of good questions."

On went the make-believe caps.

And then they focused on him. The scrutiny of twenty-some children was intense, but not as unsettling as the crystal-blue gaze of the only other adult in the room.

Miss Sunshine's eyes softened noticeably when she smiled at his daughter. "Miranda, are you ready to introduce your father?"

"Yes, I am."

He watched his daughter stand up—displaying more confidence than he was feeling at the moment—and unfold the piece of paper.

"My name is Miranda Donovan," she told the class. "My

father is a firefighter with the San Francisco Fire De—" She squinted at the page.

He leaned in to whisper it to her, but received a subtle but firm head shake from Miss Sunshine.

No helping. Got it.

"De-part-ment," she said, sounding out the word. "Department. Every day my dad goes to work and keeps people in our neighborhood safe." She wriggled a loose front tooth with her tongue. "My dad is a hero." She smiled at him then, and he thought his heart might explode.

"Is there anything else you'd like to say?" the teacher asked.

His daughter nodded and once again focused on the paper in her hand. "Please well-come…welcome…my dad, lie…oh! Lieutenant Mitchell Donovan." He would have been blown away by Miranda's poise and self-assurance if hearing her call him a hero hadn't completely knocked the air out of him. She'd never said anything like that to him before, and he wondered if maybe the teacher had suggested it.

"What a great job, Miranda. Thank you." Miss Sunshine applauded, the long bell-shaped sleeves of her hot-pink top waving like flags. The children joined in.

His daughter refolded the sheet of paper and crammed it into her pocket, and he made a mental note to retrieve it later.

For the next half hour Mitch fielded questions about hook-and-ladder trucks, dalmatians and fire poles, and why he wasn't carrying a gun. Miss Sunshine kept things on track by occasionally asking a more direct question.

Had he always wanted to be a firefighter?

For as long as he could remember.

What was the best part of the job?

Saving lives.

Was there anything about the job he didn't like?

Being too late to save a life. He couldn't say that to a bunch of little kids, though, so he simply shook his head.

He wanted to ask her if those really were little white daisies in the middle of each fuchsia-polished toe. And if that long and impossibly blond hair of hers was natural.

Once he'd managed to look past her outfit, which wasn't so much unconventional as overwhelmingly colorful, she was much more attractive than he'd originally thought. And the whole package was more than a little distracting. Especially those toes, which, for some crazy reason, he wanted to examine more closely.

The morning recess bell jolted him out of that speculation. The teacher thanked him and elicited another round of applause from her students before she dismissed them. Then the classroom cleared out faster than a fire drill. He put a hand on Miranda's shoulder, wanting to tell her how proud he was, but she jumped to her feet and slipped out of his reach.

"Me and Ashley are going to play hopscotch." She raced toward the door with the rest of the children, without even a backward glance.

And then it was just him and Miss Sunshine.

Mitch hoisted himself to his feet and flexed his legs, which had stiffened up from sitting so low to the floor.

"Sorry about the chair," she said, watching him work out the kinks. "I think it's really important for adults to work with children at their level."

Easy for her to say. He gave her a stack of fire-safety pamphlets and coloring books. "Didn't get to hand these out, but they're for the kids."

"Thank you. And I'm sorry I didn't have a chance to introduce myself when you arrived. There's never a dull moment around here." She took the books from him and extended her other hand. "I'm Rory."

Her skin was soft and cool. Her fingernails were polished to match her toes, minus the daisies, and her hands were stained with paint. Finger paint, maybe? "Good to meet you," he said. "I take it only the kids get to call you Miss Sunshine."

Her laughter lived up to the name. "My real name is Sonora Pennington-Borland, which is a bit much for the kids. My friends call me Rory. Sunshine is my…" She hesitated. "Well, it's easier for the kids and they seem to like it."

"Sounds complicated."

"You have no idea."

If her parents were anything like his, he had a *very* good idea.

"I'll be sending home permission slips today for our visit to an art gallery in a couple of weeks. I always need parent chaperones, so if you're interested…"

He had no one but himself to blame for opening that can of worms. "I'll have to check my work schedule."

"That would be great. There's a place on the permission form for you to sign up if you can join us. The children are really looking forward to seeing the abstract art exhibit. They've even been doing some of their own paintings." She indicated the bulletin boards filled with splatter art.

"Ah, yes. Very nice," he said, somewhat at a loss for words. At least this explained the paint stains on her hands.

She walked with him to the doorway and a hint of citrus wafted up as she moved—a refreshing change from the smell of chalk dust and gym shoes. Oddly enough, he was in no hurry to leave. "How long have you been teaching here?" he asked.

"This is my first year. I was born in San Francisco, but my family moved away before I started school. I grew up listening to my parents' stories about the Haight-Ashbury neighborhood and always wanted to live here, so I was really lucky to get this teaching position. I haven't found an apartment yet, but I'm looking."

So, he'd been right about her having hippie parents. Should he mention that his mother's attic apartment was empty? No. He'd already suggested she leave it vacant, and having Miranda's teacher living upstairs could get complicated. Right now, things were complicated enough. "Well, I'd better get going. Good luck with the apartment-hunting."

"Thanks."

"If you'd like to have your class visit the fire hall sometime, give me a call," he said, surprising himself.

"Really? Thank you. The kids would love it. Field trips are such a great way to expose them to new things. And it's so good to meet parents who are involved in their children's education."

"Like I said, anytime." He felt like a fraud, though, and he hoped he wouldn't get found out. "Um…I guess I should give you my number."

She handed him a pen and held out one of the pamphlets he'd given her.

He scrawled his cell phone number on the cover. He couldn't remember the last time he'd given his phone number to a woman.

"Great, thanks." She smiled up at him when he handed the pen back.

Oh, God, he thought. Did she think he was hitting on her? Maybe he should tell her he wasn't.

Sure, because women always liked to hear that.

"Recess is almost over," she said. "Thanks again for

coming. Miranda has talked nonstop about having you here."

His daughter had been in second grade for all of two weeks and she had also talked endlessly about her new teacher. The invitation to speak to the class had come out of the blue, and it was only his daughter's unrestrained enthusiasm that had prompted him to accept. Now he was glad he had. Kids needed parents who were involved, and his involvement was long overdue.

RORY TURNED OFF Haight Street and found a parking spot halfway down the steeply sloped street. She eased her van into it and yanked on the emergency brake. "Come on, Vanna. This is not the place to let me down," she said, slowly easing her foot off the brake pedal. The van stayed where it was. She gently tapped the steering wheel. "Thank you."

She dug a slip of paper out of her book bag and checked the address her mother's friend had written down for her. This was the place. She turned off the ignition and waited for the engine to stop sputtering before she stepped out and looked up at the house.

It was a classic San Francisco Victorian—two and a half stories with a garage entrance to the basement. This one had been painted bright yellow and accented with two shades of blue that set off the gingerbread trim. The blue house with red-and-gold trim next door appeared to be its twin, except the front door and bay window were on opposite sides. They were separated by a narrow walkway that led to the backyard, a rare feature in this neighborhood.

She hadn't exaggerated when she'd told Mitch Donovan that she'd spent most of her life wanting to live in the neighborhood her parents always reminisced about with so much affection. She could hardly believe that everything had come together so perfectly. She'd landed the ideal teaching position, and now she had a chance to have an apartment in one of these wonderful old houses. Could the life of a confirmed single woman be any more perfect?

She climbed the front steps, exchanged grins with a quirky clay dragon on the top step and rang the bell. Music drifted out of the house, so someone must be home. She rang the bell again and tapped her foot to Van Morrison's "Brown-Eyed Girl" while she waited. Her mother had that record—a real vinyl one, come to think of it—and Rory must have heard it a hundred times.

The door was finally opened by a tall, robust-looking woman wearing a baggy gray sweatshirt and a pair of faded denim shorts. "Can I help you?" she asked. The sweatshirt was mud-spattered and she was wiping her hands on an old towel. She must be a potter, Rory deduced. Her mother's neighbor in Mendocino was a potter, and he was always covered with clay.

"Hi. I'm Rory." She tentatively extended her hand. "My friend Annie McGaskell told me you have an apartment for rent."

"Of course. She sent an e-mail to say you'd be stopping by. Nice to meet you. I'm Betsy Evans." She gave Rory a vigorous handshake. "Follow me. The apartment's on the top floor."

Betsy's dark brown hair hung in a single braid down her back, and it swung from side to side as she climbed the creaky staircase. Varicose veins snaked up the backs of her lightly tanned calves. "I hope you're okay with stairs," she said. "There are two flights."

"Not a problem." Rory was puffing by the time they reached the top floor, though, and a little chagrined that her prospective landlady wasn't.

"Don't worry," Betsy said. "After a few weeks of these

stairs and walking up and down the hills in this neighborhood, you'll be in great shape. The house has two staircases, by the way. We use the one at the back of the house, so you'll have this one all to yourself. The door on the second-floor landing is locked from both sides, so you'll have complete privacy."

"That's great," Rory said. "I've always loved these old houses."

"Me, too. I've lived here a long time, since before my kids were born, and I'm now a grandmother."

"Really? My parents and I used to live in this neighborhood, but we moved up the coast to Mendocino when I was four or five."

From a small landing at the top of the staircase, Betsy opened another door. "Here we are. The apartment is really just one big open space plus the bathroom, but it's completely self-contained. It's partly furnished, but I can have everything taken out if you don't need it."

Rory stepped inside and instantly fell in love with it. "It's wonderful," she said. "I wouldn't change a thing."

The apartment was perfect. Bright and spacious, and in spite of the sloped ceilings, there would be plenty of room to hang her mother's paintings. There were even built-in shelves for all the books her father kept sending her.

Betsy was right—it was really just one big room that ran the full length of the house. The sleeping area overlooked the street and the kitchen was at the back. The living area, with an assortment of shabby-chic furniture, was in the middle. The walls were a light buttery yellow with gleaming white trim around the doors and windows. The distressed wood floors had been painted dark gray with a red, yellow and blue folk-art design stenciled around the living-room area, setting it off from the rest of the space.

"Did you paint the floor yourself?"

"I did. Do you like it?"

"I love it." She peeked into the bathroom. It had yellow wainscoting and white fixtures and she loved the retro look of the black-and-white ceramic floor tiles, which were so perfect with the old-fashioned pedestal sink and clawfoot bathtub.

Betsy walked to the far end of the space. "There's a Murphy bed in here," she said, pointing to a wall unit. "It was the most efficient way to use the space, and when it's open, it's right under the skylight."

"What a great idea." Rory could imagine herself lying in bed, gazing up at the stars and trying to figure out which constellation she could see.

The kitchen area overlooked the backyard.

"There's enough room on the balcony for a chair or two. The last tenant even had a little barbecue out there."

Rory peered through the glass-paned door and shuddered. She had no intention of sitting out there, never mind cooking, three stories above the ground. It would be an ideal place for a few potted geraniums, though, and for Buick to soak up the sun.

"Oh, I hope you don't mind that I have a cat," Rory said. "He's old and lazy and he stays inside all the time, but he'll love the balcony."

"I don't mind at all. Now tell me, how do you know Annie?"

"She's an old friend of my mother's. I've been staying with her since I moved to San Francisco a couple of weeks ago, but her apartment is *very* small."

"It is that, all right. Annie and I have been friends for years, too. I wonder if I know your mother."

"You might—her name is Copper Pennington."

"You don't say! I haven't seen Copper in years, but I've

been following her career. Doesn't she have a show later this month?"

"In two weeks. Annie and I are going to the opening. You're welcome to join us."

"I'd love to," Betsy said. "So, what do you think of the apartment?"

"It's perfect. When is it available?"

"Right away, and it's yours if you want it."

"Really? Thank you! Annie told me how much the rent is. Would you like me to fill out an application and give you a deposit?"

"Heavens, no. Any friend of Annie's is a friend of mine. We can look after the money when you move in. Do you know when that'll be?"

Rory was tempted to say right now, but that wasn't practical. "Would Saturday morning be okay?"

"It would. I'll be sure there's someone here to help you carry your things upstairs."

"I should be able to manage," Rory said, although after several trips up and down those stairs, she'd probably wish she didn't have so many books and clothes. And shoes. And purses.

"It's no problem. Come on downstairs and I'll get the key for you."

Five minutes later, Rory was back in her van with the key to her new apartment dangling from her key chain. All the karma her mother said she'd been storing up was finally paying off.

The fire-safety book with Mitch Donovan's phone number still lay where she'd tossed it on the passenger seat. The messages he'd been sending out that afternoon had definitely been mixed. *Here's my number.* But then it seemed as though he was thinking *please don't call.* And now she *had* to call, but for all the wrong reasons.

One of the boys in the class had shoved Miranda off the steps during afternoon recess and she had retaliated. Although neither child had been badly hurt, it was school policy to talk to the parents when these things happened.

Since she'd moved to the city a couple of weeks ago, Mitch was the first *interesting* man she'd met—and calling him to arrange a class field trip would have been the perfect excuse to talk to him again. Calling to tell him his daughter had misbehaved...not so much.

There was a very good chance that he was spoken for, she reminded herself. At least, she assumed he was still married to Miranda's mother, even though the way he'd looked at her suggested he was either single or would like to be.

Single or not, she had noticed that he had great hands, and there'd been no wedding band. She'd learned the hard way to pay attention to details like that. Not that the absence of a ring meant a man was single—another lesson learned the hard way.

Would a firefighter wear a ring while he was on duty? Maybe not. And now that she thought about it, Miranda often spoke about her father but she'd never mentioned her mother. The details were probably in Miranda's permanent file, but she hadn't read any of her students' files. She preferred to get to know them on her terms. Miranda was bright and creative, but at times she was moody and unpredictable. This afternoon had been one of those times. Maybe she should look at Miranda's file tomorrow. A quick peek couldn't hurt.

She picked up the fire-safety pamphlet and took a closer look. The numbers he'd written on the cover were large and neatly formed. A man's hands—and his handwriting—said a lot about who he was, so she always paid attention to them. Mitch had strong hands with long, perfectly proportioned fingers. While he had sat in her classroom on a too-small chair with his very long legs extended into the circle, he hadn't looked the least bit self-conscious. His hands had rested lightly on his thighs, steady and unmoving, except for the few times he had lifted one or both to demonstrate something to her students. Even then, they had moved with purpose, and then they'd deliberately returned to their resting place on those hard, muscular thighs.

You don't know they were hard and muscular.

"Oh, yes, I do." It would take more than a dark navy SFFD uniform to disguise what was clearly the product of a dedicated workout regime.

In the commotion that ensued after the recess bell had rung, he had gently placed one of those big hands on his daughter's shoulder. It had been a tender, fleeting gesture, more than a little protective, and Rory's heart had melted just a little bit.

She set the pamphlet back on the seat next to her and slipped the key into the ignition. Her cell phone rang then, and her friend Nicola's name and number appeared on the call display. She loved Nic dearly but she only ever called when she needed something, and Rory already knew what that was. "Hi, Nic. What's up?"

"Rory! Did you get my text message?"

"Ah, no." She glanced quickly at the display screen on her phone, then put it back to her ear. "This is a new phone and I haven't figured out all the functions yet."

"Really? Texting is so easy."

"I'm sure it is."

"Anyway, I'm *so* glad I caught you. I need you to block off Saturday afternoon. I've arranged for the five of us to go into the shop for dress fittings."

"I just rented an apartment. I'm moving on Saturday."

"Where is it?"

"Just off Haight Street, maybe three blocks from the school. It's perfect."

Her friend laughed. "You really are your mother's daughter."

"That's me, all right. Living the dream."

"Do you think moving will take all day? I've already booked the seamstress for two o'clock. If you need help, I can send Jonathan over."

Rory laughed. Jonathan would do anything for Nicola, even if it meant schlepping her friend's belongings up two flights of stairs. "That's okay. My landlady said someone will be here to help, and I don't have that much stuff."

And I'll have Saturday evening and all day Sunday to get settled, Rory reminded herself.

"That's great. So you'll be free by two? I can't do this without my maid of honor."

"I'll be there." Rory dug a pen and notepad out of her bag. "What's the address?"

She scribbled it onto a blank page while Nicola continued talking.

"Jess's part-time bartender is filling in for her at The Whiskey Sour. After the fittings we'll all head over there for appies, drinks, girl talk, the whole nine yards. My treat."

Now *that* sounded like fun. It had been ages since the five of them had spent an afternoon together. "Count me in. Is Maria coming to the bar, too?"

"Of course. Being pregnant doesn't mean she can't have a little fun. She'll just have to drink milk or something. Oh, and wait till you see the dresses. They're a gorgeous shade of periwinkle blue, and I even found a style that will work for everyone and be easily altered to accommodate Maria's baby bump. Isn't that great?"

Rory ran a hand over her own perfectly flat stomach and tried to picture herself in a gown that could be *easily altered* to accommodate a bridesmaid who'd be almost seven months pregnant by the day of the wedding. Maybe Nic was thinking this was her chance for a payback. At Maria's wedding, the four bridesmaids could have been plucked off a cotton-candy stand at a carnival. At Paige's, they had resembled a small forest of Christmas trees. Now it was…what…Goodyear Blimp time?

How could these intelligent and otherwise sensible women have such bad taste when it came to dressing their bridesmaids? On the bright side, she only had to be a bridesmaid one more time, providing Jess let down her guard long enough to let a man into her life.

"Listen, sweetie, I have a million things to do," Nic said. "Have to run, but I'll see you on Saturday."

"See you then. Bye." Rory tucked her phone into her bag and glanced up at the house one more time. In the big scheme of things, being a bridesmaid wasn't so bad. She only had to put up with a bad dress for one day—and avoid catching one more bouquet. Not such a big deal, since life as a single woman in San Francisco was turning out to be pretty much everything she'd hoped for.

Chapter Two

In the grocery-store parking lot, Mitch held the rear car door open for his daughter, and, after she climbed into her booster seat, he tried to help her buckle the seat belt.

She snatched it out of his hand. "Dad! I can do it myself."

"I know you can, princess. I'm just trying to help." But she was right, and her protest brought Miss Sunshine's silent reprimand to mind.

No helping.

On some level he knew that, but the need to do things for Miranda and be sure they were done right was not easy to overcome. As she fumbled with the seat belt, he noticed a tear in her jeans. "What happened to your knee?"

She slapped a hand over the hole. "Nothing."

"It doesn't look like nothing."

"I fell, okay?"

His inclination to reprimand her for being disrespectful was overshadowed by concern for her well-being. "Did you hurt yourself?"

"Da-ad! Just drop it. It's no big deal."

Let it go, he told himself, resisting the urge to roll up her pant leg and make sure she really was okay. He reluctantly closed the door and walked around to the back of his SUV. He'd picked up Miranda after school and they'd stopped to buy the things on the list his mother had given him. As he loaded bags of groceries into the back, two college-aged women walked by, all coy smiles and making a point of catching his eye. Apparently they hadn't noticed the child sitting in the backseat.

After making brief eye contact with one of them, he quickly looked away. He had enough of an ego to realize it wasn't *all* the uniform, but mostly it was. Other than going to work, he rarely wore it in public, and this was why. The uniform did not blend into a crowd, and that's all he wanted to do. Blend in and get by. People kept saying things would get easier, but so far, those people were wrong.

And, as if he didn't feel lousy enough already, he had to toss in a healthy measure of guilt. He'd sat in Miranda's classroom that morning and lusted after a pair of feet. What the hell had that been about? For the life of him, he couldn't conjure up an image of Laura's feet, and he couldn't ever remember thinking they were sexy.

If he were being honest, he'd lusted after more than the feet today, but guilt seemed to do strange things to a guy's ability to be honest. He was just having a normal reaction to a beautiful woman. Still, he shouldn't have given her his phone number, and he shouldn't be secretly hoping she'd call. He got behind the wheel, did up his own seat belt and pulled out of the parking lot.

Mind you, he told himself, *there's a lot of territory between admiring a woman's assets and acquiring them.* Besides, he had his daughter to think about. He couldn't imagine telling Miranda that he was interested in a woman who wasn't her mother. How could a seven-year-old even begin to understand something like that?

"Can we go for ice cream before we go home?" Miranda asked, her annoyance over his questions about the ripped jeans already forgotten.

"Sorry, princess. Not today. We need to get these groceries home to Grams before dinnertime."

Little girls were terrible at hiding their disappointment, and his daughter was no exception.

"Tell you what," he said. "Saturday's my day off. We'll go down to Fisherman's Wharf and have ice cream, just like we used to. Make a whole day of it."

Maybe if they did something Laura used to love doing, some of his guilt would go away.

Miranda's eyes lit up. "Can we take the cable car?"

No, he wanted to say. Going to the wharf felt like a big enough first step. "We'll see," he said. Maybe by Saturday she'd forget about the cable car.

Even as he thought it, he knew the chances were nil. He'd have to come up with an excuse, though. Some things he simply wasn't ready for, and riding the cable cars was one of them.

At home he pulled into the narrow driveway and pushed the remote for the garage door. They drove in, and his mother came out of her studio to meet them.

"Perfect timing," she said. "I just finished up for the day."

Between the three of them, they hauled the grocery bags up the stairs and deposited them on the kitchen table. As Mitch started unloading the contents, his mother picked up a small timer and set it.

"Something smells good. What are you cooking?" he asked.

"There's a brown-rice-and-lentil casserole in the oven and a salad in the fridge."

All organic, no doubt. He hoped Miranda would eat it without making a fuss.

"This isn't for the stove, though. I'm reminding myself to check the kiln later and make sure it shuts off."

"Is there a problem with it?"

"No. It's new, and I want to be sure it's working properly."

There had been a kiln in this basement for as long as he could remember—since before he was born, actually—and he'd always taken for granted that it worked properly. Now that he'd moved back here with Miranda, it was good to know the equipment was new and reliable.

"Oh, good news," his mother said, shaking her head at the box of cereal she'd hauled out of one of the bags. "I rented the attic apartment this afternoon."

"I thought you'd decided to leave it vacant."

"No, that's what *you* decided I should do."

"I told you I'll take care of expenses now that Miranda and I are living here." He hated the idea of having a stranger living in the house with his daughter. His mother no longer needed the money, but she had an independent streak a mile wide, and that meant not letting anyone look after her.

"Who's moving in?" he asked.

"A friend of Annie's. Actually, the daughter of a friend of Annie's."

"But you still checked her references, right?"

"Didn't have to."

"Because…?"

"Because she's the daughter of a friend of Annie's."

He couldn't believe his mother was so trusting. "How do we know this person will be a good influence on Miranda?"

"She won't be living with us—she'll be in the attic apartment."

"You know what I mean."

"Oh, I know what you mean, all right, but last time I checked, it was a human rights violation to refuse to rent an apartment to someone because my son questioned her moral fiber."

Mitch cared about only one human's rights, and those were Miranda's. "Does she have a job?"

"I assume so."

"You didn't ask?"

"No. Annie wouldn't have sent her if she was a deadbeat."

God help him, but there were days when he wondered if his mother was a good influence on Miranda. Maybe he should have told Miss Sunshine about the apartment. It would have been better to have her living here than a complete stranger.

"She's moving in on Saturday morning. I told her you'd help move her things upstairs."

Gee, thanks.

"Me and Dad are going to Fisherman's Wharf on Saturday," Miranda announced. She was polishing apples on her shirt, just the way her mother used to, and setting them in the fruit bowl, so she missed her grandmother's reaction.

Mitch put the milk in the fridge and tried to ignore the feel of his mother's gaze boring into his back.

"That'll be fun," she said. "I don't think you've been there since your mother died."

Mitch felt his spine go rigid. *Dead, died, death.* He *hated* those words. No seven-year-old needed to hear them, especially about her mother, but his mother had no trouble using them. *Tell it like it is,* that was her mantra.

Miranda, still filling the fruit bowl, seemed unfazed by her grandmother's directness.

Helping the new tenant move upstairs would take up at least half the day. He and Miranda could still spend the afternoon at the wharf, but there definitely wouldn't be time for a cable-car ride.

His mother picked up Miranda's backpack. "Can you run this up to your room so I can set the table?"

"'Kay." She flung the bag over her shoulder and was headed out of the room when Betsy stopped her.

"What happened to your jeans? Is that a hole in the knee?"

Miranda swung around, instantly defiant. "I already *told* Dad that I fell at school. It was an accident."

"Miranda! That is no way to talk to your grandmother."

"Sorry." But she still looked more insolent than contrite. "I didn't mean to rip them."

"No problem," Betsy said. "When you take them off, fold them up and put them on the chair in your room. When I have some time, I'll mend them for you."

Instead of agreeing, Miranda marched out of the room and up the stairs.

"Sorry about that," he said to his mother after he heard his daughter's footsteps in the hallway upstairs. "I don't know what's bugging her today."

"She's had to make a lot of adjustments in the past couple of weeks. New home, new school, new friends. She'll settle down once she's had a chance to get used to everything."

He sure hoped so. "Do you need some help with dinner?"

"If you'll set the table, I'll mix up some salad dressing."

He was taking plates out of the cupboard when his cell phone rang. He set the dishes on the table and pulled the phone out of his pocket. The number on the call display wasn't familiar but he answered it anyway.

"Hello?"

"Hi, Mitch?"

"Yes?"

"Hi. This is Rory. Miranda's teacher."

He'd known who it was as soon as she'd said hello. "Hi." He'd been hoping she would call, but he hadn't dared to hope it would happen this soon.

"There was a bit of a…well…an incident at school this afternoon. Maybe Miranda has already spoken to you about it?"

His thoughts went immediately to the ripped jeans. "No, she hasn't. Nothing serious, I hope."

"Serious enough," she said. "She and one of the boys in the class got into a squabble during afternoon recess. Franklin pushed Miranda off the stairs, and Miranda tore her jeans and scraped her knee."

"I noticed that, but when I asked her about it, she said she fell."

"I thought she might not tell you what happened. That's why I called to talk to you."

"I appreciate the call." What he didn't understand was why Miranda hadn't told him about it herself.

"Unfortunately, there's more. Miranda got up and pushed him back."

Mitch flashed back to his own childhood days on the playground. He hated to think of anyone pushing his daughter around, but he was glad to hear she could stand up for herself. "I guess kids will be kids."

That was met with silence.

"Are you still there?" he asked.

"I am. I was hoping you and Miranda's mother would talk to her about this behavior, and about the appropriate way to handle disputes." Her voice had taken on the same calm, cool tone she'd used that morning when she'd spoken to her students about putting on their thinking caps and their best manners. "Even though the other child pushed her first, she shouldn't have pushed him back. There's always a supervisor on the playground during recess and children need to ask for help when a situation gets out of hand and to learn that it's inappropriate to take matters into their own hands."

Give me a break. "These kids are seven years old. Fighting back seems like a pretty natural reaction when—"

"Mr. Donovan. The school has zero tolerance when it comes to bullying and aggressiveness. It doesn't matter who starts a fight."

So now it was Mr. Donovan. "It sounds to me like Miranda's the one who's being bullied. Shouldn't you be calling Franklin's parents?"

"I already have. I wanted to let both of you know what happened so you can discuss it with your children and help them come up with a strategy for dealing with these kinds of situations."

Seven-year-olds were supposed to have strategies? "Fine, I'll talk to her…" As soon as he figured out what the hell kind of strategy she needed.

"Thank you," she said. "My door is always open. If you ever have questions or concerns about anything that's going on at school, feel free to come in and talk to me."

So she could tell him to his face that he was doing a lousy job of raising his daughter? Not going to happen.

"Thanks," he said. "Is there anything else?"

"No. Goodb—"

He ended the call before she finished and shoved the phone back into his pocket. His mother had finished setting the table and was taking the casserole out of the oven. She looked at him questioningly. "Everything okay?" she asked.

"That was the teacher. Miranda got into a fight at school today."

"That explains the torn jeans."

"I wonder why she didn't tell me what happened."

His mother laughed. "She didn't want to get in trouble."

"But if some kid's picking on her—"

"Is that what the teacher said?"

Mitch relayed the story, then he shrugged, still at a bit of a loss. "The teacher says I need to help her come up with a coping strategy."

"That's easy enough."

It was?

Betsy took the casserole out of the oven and set it on a trivet on the counter. "I agree with Miss Sunshine. Physical violence is never the answer. If someone's picking on Miranda, she needs to ask for help. It's too easy for situations like this to get out of control, and the next thing you know, someone gets hurt."

Good point. That was the last thing he wanted to happen to his daughter. "Can we hold dinner for a few minutes? I'll go up and talk to her right now." He might as well get it over with.

"Take all the time you need. I'll just pop this back in the oven and keep it warm."

"Thanks." He still thought everyone was overreacting, and he sure as hell resented the implication that Miranda was a troublemaker. However, he didn't ever want her to end up in a situation that put her at risk.

"What are you going to say to her?"

"Pretty much what you just said, I guess." He'd never been any good at these sorts of things, which was why he'd always let Laura handle them.

TWO DAYS LATER, Mitch arrived home from his night shift at the fire hall, dog-tired but in time to help his daughter get ready for school. Her teacher was once again the topic of conversation. When he'd talked to Miranda about the playground fight with Franklin, he had done his best to conceal his resentment over Rory's criticism. Miranda, he quickly discovered, harbored no ill feelings toward her teacher whatsoever. She had simply declared that all boys, Franklin in particular, were poo-heads, and then she'd readily agreed to talk to a teacher if anyone tried to pick on her again. He'd been left feeling that what he didn't know about parenting was only surpassed by what he didn't know about little girls.

"Miss Sunshine's been teaching us how to hopscotch."

"That's nice, but if you don't hold still until I finish brushing your hair, you'll be late for school and Ror...um, Ms. Pennington-Borland..." He felt silly calling her Miss Sunshine but using her first name didn't seem right, either. "Your teacher will suspend your playground privileges."

Miranda laughed. "She would *never* do that. She's super nice. When I grow up, I'm going to be a teacher just like her."

"Good for you." Mitch worked the last tangle out of his daughter's blond curls and planted a kiss on the top of her head. "There you go. For now you'll have to settle for being the prettiest girl in second grade."

"Do you think Miss Sunshine is pretty?"

Yes, he did. He also knew that if he told Miranda, then Ms. Pennington-Borland would know, too, and he couldn't see any advantage to that. "I didn't notice," he said.

"When you get married again, I think you should marry her."

Dumbfounded, Mitch met his daughter's gaze in the mirror. "What makes you think I'll get married again?"

"So you can be happy. And so I can have a mom who knows how to hopscotch."

His gut tightened. At least she hadn't said she wanted

another mom who loved to ride the cable cars. "I'm happy."

"You don't smile."

He forced his mouth to do what his daughter claimed it didn't. "I'm happy, princess. I promise." Mitch set the hairbrush on his daughter's dresser. "I'll bet Grams is downstairs, waiting to walk you to school."

"When will I be able to walk by myself?"

Gee, let's see. Never? She was his reason for getting up every morning, and he intended to do everything in his power to see that nothing terrible ever happened to her. "Is your backpack ready to go?" he asked, deciding to ignore the question. This time it worked.

"Yup. It's by the front door. Did you sign my permission slip for the art gallery field trip?"

"I did," he said. "It's stuck on the door of the fridge."

"Did you say you'll be a chaperone?"

"I did." He wasn't sure why, exactly, since Miss Sunshine didn't seem to think much of his parenting skills, and since neither modern art nor a mob of second graders held any appeal. But it was what Laura would have done, and it was time he started being more involved in their daughter's life.

After Miranda dashed downstairs, he remembered the page with her speech that she had put in her pocket when he'd visited her classroom. Her torn jeans were still folded on the seat of her chair and sure enough, there it was. He unfolded the piece of paper and read it. Most of the words sounded like hers, but the printing wasn't. He could imagine Miss Rory Sonora Sunshine Pennington whatever—man, how many names did one person need?—sitting on one of those little chairs next to his daughter, smiling her encouragement and patiently copying down the words she wanted to say.

Despite being a father, he didn't have much experience with children, but he had enough to know that Miranda was often a little too quiet, a bit on the moody side and far too serious for a seven-year-old. Right now she lived with an eccentric grandmother who had never quite managed to leave the sixties behind and a father who had, by all reports, forgotten how to smile. She could use a strong, positive influence in her life. Would he have chosen a high-spirited teacher who was clearly the product of a couple of misguided hippies herself? No. But in spite of his own uncertainty when it came to Miss Sunshine, he had a feeling she might be just what Miranda needed right now.

ON SATURDAY MORNING, Rory woke to the sound of her cell phone ringing. She opened one sleepy eye and peered at the clock. Ugh. This was the last morning she'd wake up on the sofa bed in Annie's tiny living room, and she had a big day ahead of her.

Moving into her new apartment.

A dress fitting.

Dinner and drinks with the girls.

Even so, she hadn't planned to be up *this* early. Neither had her cat. He hoisted himself off her feet and looked very annoyed as she shifted and grabbed her phone off the coffee table. It was her father.

"Hi, Dad? It's awfully early. Is everything okay?"

"Sorry, sugar. I always forget about the time difference."

"No problem. You know I love to hear from you." The cat arched his back, turned around twice and settled back onto her feet.

"I got an e-mail from your mother. She said you found a place in the old neighborhood, so I'm calling to wish you a happy housewarming."

"Thanks, Dad." She was constantly amazed that her parents still communicated. Maybe they should have used e-mail when they were married. Of course, being separated by an entire continent didn't hurt, either. "It's a gorgeous old house, half a block off Haight Street and really close to the school. I have the attic apartment, and Betsy—she's my landlord and a friend of Annie's, and she even knows Mom—has the rest of the house."

"Sounds wonderful, Rory. And how's your new job working out?"

"I love it. My students are awesome, and the school's great." The day before classes had started, she'd walked through each classroom, imagining herself there as a kid. "And I'm so happy the girls and I are finally living in the same city again."

"That's right. How are they?"

"Jess is the same as ever, Maria's baby is due in a couple of months, Paige and her husband are separated, and Nicola's getting married. We're getting together this afternoon to have our bridesmaids' dresses fitted. What's new with you?"

"The latest book is doing well."

That was an understatement. "How many bestseller lists have you hit with this one?"

"Oh, one or two." He never mentioned them unless she asked. He was genuinely modest about his success, and it was one of the things she admired most about him.

"The reviews have been fantastic, Dad."

"You've been following them?"

"Of course I have! When's your book tour?"

"We leave on Monday."

She wondered if he'd tell her what he meant by *we* or if he'd make her ask. "You're coming to San Francisco, I hope."

"I haven't seen my itinerary yet. My assistant is handling those details."

And there was her answer. Her father had a thing about assistants. Especially young female assistants. Rory didn't know if he started dating these women and then hired them, or vice versa. Either way, they never lasted.

"How old is this one?" she asked.

He chuckled at that. "Older than you."

She didn't ask by how much. "I'm looking forward to meeting her." What else could she say?

"What about you?" he asked. "Seeing anyone?"

An image of a tall and seriously good-looking firefighter flashed into Rory's mind, which was crazy. He was the father of one of her students and most likely married. Which reminded her, in spite of everything that had transpired this week, that she'd forgotten to look at Miranda's file. "No, Dad, I'm not. I had a busy summer, and then there was the move here and getting settled into a new school. You'll just have to get used to having a daughter who's an old maid."

She laughed and so did he.

"Still sworn off kids and commitment, I see."

She preferred to think of it as swearing off all the chaos and emotional turmoil that went with the kind of commitment he was talking about. Kids she could handle, but marriage? No way. "May I remind you that I haven't had the best role models?"

More laughter. She could joke about this with him. With her mother, not so much.

"I look forward to meeting the guy who finally changes your mind."

Like that was going to happen. "Give it up, Dad. Not going to happen."

"I'm a patient man, sugar."

"Enough of your sweet talk. You'll call as soon as you know when…if…you'll be in San Francisco?"

"Of course. You can reintroduce me to Haight-Ashbury, and I'll take you out for dinner."

She wanted to ask if it could be just the two of them, but that would sound childish. "Hope to see you soon, Dad. Love you."

"Love you, too, Rory. Have fun today, and say hi to the girls for me."

"You bet. Bye."

She set her phone on the coffee table and glanced around the tiny living room. It had been very generous of Annie to let her stay here while she looked for an apartment, but this place was barely big enough for one person, let alone two plus an overweight cat. She wriggled her toes under the big black-and-white ball of fur curled on top of her feet. "Time to get up, sleepyhead. It's moving day."

MITCH WAS UP EARLY on Saturday morning. He had always liked weekend mornings, especially when they coincided with his days off. When Laura was alive, the three of them would have a leisurely breakfast and then head out for the day. After the accident it had been all he could do to drag himself out of bed in the morning. Looking back, taking an extended leave of absence had been a bad decision. Not nearly as bad as shift work, though, and having to leave Miranda with a series of irresponsible babysitters who spent most of their time on the phone, or with a nanny who turned out to have a taste for vodka.

Much as he loved his mother, moving back into her place wasn't an ideal situation, either. He'd always said he would never live in this neighborhood again, but this arrangement meant that when he was at work overnight, Miranda was well cared for and he didn't need to worry about her. Or at least he worried less.

Starting today, he decided, things would be different. His mother had gone to the park with her tai chi group, so he and Miranda were on their own for breakfast. After he helped the new tenant move in, he and his daughter would spend the afternoon at Fisherman's Wharf. Miranda would love it, but it also felt like the right thing to do to honor his wife. Strangely enough, that hadn't seemed necessary until he'd met his daughter's teacher. Being attracted to another woman was sure as hell *not* the way to honor Laura.

He filled two bowls with cereal and topped them up with milk. No match for Laura's blueberry waffles, but it was a start.

"Here you go," he said, sliding a bowl in front of Miranda.

She sat across the table from him, still wearing her favorite pink Sponge Bob pajamas. They were getting too small, he noticed. One of these days he should take her shopping.

Or he could ask his mother to take her.

No, he should do it.

Miranda wiggled her loose tooth between spoonfuls of cereals. "When we go on the cable car today, I want to stand up and ride on the outside."

Mitch's spoon paused halfway to his mouth. "I'm pretty sure they don't let kids your age do that. It's too dangerous. Besides, somebody's moving into the apartment this morning and Grams asked me to stick around and give her a hand. We might only have enough time to go the wharf."

His daughter eyed him over the rim of her cereal bowl. "You don't want to ride on a cable car, do you?"

No. Yes. No, he didn't, but damn it, how did a seven-year-old get to be so perceptive? What would Laura have done in a situation like this?

Tell her the truth.

He couldn't be sure if that was Laura's voice in his head or Miss Sunshine's, but honesty was probably the best way to go. If he told her the truth, maybe she'd drop it, at least for now.

"No," he said. "Not really."

"Is it because of Mom?"

He hadn't seen that coming, either. Did he want to be completely honest? "Yes," he said finally. "It is."

On their first date, he'd taken Laura for a cable-car ride and she'd loved it. Six months later he'd proposed to her on one, and a year after that, it was where she'd told him they were going to have a baby. Not that he was overly sentimental, but he associated the city's cable cars with being in love, not with grieving, and he wanted to keep it that way.

"That's kind of dumb, don't you think?"

"Excuse me?"

"Mom's not here anymore, but she'd still want us to be having fun."

Mitch set his spoon in his bowl. There was no sense putting anything in his mouth, since he'd never be able to swallow it anyway. He was the parent, yet there were times when his daughter seemed way more sensible. "You're right," he said, although he still wasn't saying yes to the cable car. "The wharf and some ice cream will be fun. I'll bet you even know what flavor you want."

"Uh-huh. Chocolate-chip cookie dough."

Mitch shuddered—even the name grossed him out—but he didn't let on to Miranda. "I knew you'd say that."

"And you'll have chocolate," she said confidently. "You always do."

She was right. Laura had tried something different every time, but he was a creature of habit. There was nothing wrong with wanting things to stay the same, forever— except for having to deal with the devastation when they didn't.

He watched Miranda pick up her bowl and drink the last of her milk and soggy cereal. Laura, in spite of her spirit of adventure, would have reminded her to use her manners, and a spoon. Like Miss Sunshine having her students put on their best manners.

He gave his head a shake. It had been well over a year since Laura's accident, and for the past few months he'd been getting by just fine. Some nights he'd go to bed and realize he hadn't thought about her all day. On the one hand he felt guilty, but on the other he thought he was finally pulling his life back together. Or at least managing to live it. But since he'd met Rory Pennington-Borland, the guilt was back in spades, and so were all these haunting thoughts about Laura.

He didn't know who to blame. Laura, for leaving him? Rory, for having those ridiculously sexy feet? Or himself, for being so weak? The answer was a no-brainer. It wasn't Rory's fault, and being angry with his dead wife made no sense.

Miranda's spoon clanged into her empty bowl. "I'm going upstairs to pick out what I'm going to wear this afternoon."

Mitch stacked their bowls and put them in the sink. "Need some help?"

"Nope," she said. "I can do it myself."

He let her go. He was rinsing their dishes and loading them into the dishwasher when the doorbell rang. He glanced at the clock. If this was the new tenant, she was an early bird.

He opened the front door and stared at the woman standing there. "Miss Sunshine?"

Great. Now she was making house calls to point out what a lousy parent he was.

Chapter Three

Before Mitch could stop himself, he glanced down at Rory's feet. *Idiot,* he chided himself. But to his relief, they were sensibly clad in a pair of hand-painted white sneakers. Okay, maybe not so sensible. Beside those sat a small pet carrier stuffed with a large quantity of black and white fur. And then the reality of why she was here settled into his consciousness with a tangible thud.

She was the new tenant.

"Hi," she said. At first she looked just as surprised to see him, then she laughed. "I rented Betsy's attic apartment," she said, pointing up the stairs. "So…is she your mother?"

He nodded.

"Wow," she said. "This is a surprise."

More like a bombshell. Just what he needed. His daughter's teacher—her very attractive teacher who seemed to think he was a less-than-stellar parent—living right upstairs.

"Betsy said there'd be someone here to help carry my things upstairs. Did she mean you?"

"That's what she meant." *Thanks, Mom.*

"I really appreciate it," she said, and she seemed sincere. "This place has a *lot* of stairs."

"How much stuff do you have?" he asked, wondering what he'd been volunteered for.

"My van is packed pretty full," she said, pointing over her shoulder in the direction of the street. "That's everything, though, and it's mostly…you know…stuff. Not much furniture."

He looked past her. "*That* van?" The ancient two-tone green Volkswagen with a kaleidoscope of flowers painted down the side?

She nodded. "It used to be my mother's. Pretty cool, huh?"

Groovy.

Miranda appeared and saved him having to answer out loud. "Miss Sunshine!" she squealed.

"Hi, Miranda." Rory glanced at his daughter, still in her too-small pajamas, and then back up at him. "So…do you two actually *live* here?"

"We do," Mitch said. That seemed to genuinely surprise her, which meant that in addition to not checking references, his mother hadn't exchanged any personal information with her. No surprise there.

"You're who's moving into the attic apartment?" Miranda asked.

"That's right. We'll be neighbors."

"That's so awesome. Wait'll I tell the kids at school." She crouched in front of the overstuffed pet carrier. "Who's this?"

Rory knelt beside her. "My cat. His name is Buick."

"Can I pet him?"

"You sure can, but let's take him upstairs first. I don't want to open his crate down here because he'll probably run away."

They both stood up. "I can help you move in, too," Miranda said. "I'm good at helping."

"I know you are. Thank you for offering."

Mitch glanced down at his daughter and smoothed a hand over her feathery curls. "Run upstairs and get dressed, okay? Ro—um, Miss Sun—" Man, this was going to be awkward. "We'll get started."

"'Kay. I'll be back in a flash."

That made his chest tighten. Laura used to say that all the time. *Back in a flash,* she'd written on the note she'd left that day when she'd gone to pick up Miranda from a birthday party, in case he got home before they returned. Except she hadn't returned, and by the time he'd found the note, he already knew she never would. The only thing he could be grateful for was that the accident had happened on her way to the party, and their daughter hadn't been in the car with her.

Rory laughed as she watched Miranda run up the stairs. "She's adorable. So much energy and creativity. I love having her in my class."

"That's not the impression I got when you called the other day."

Her laughter faded and she looked at him with narrowed eyes. "I'm sorry you were offended." Except she didn't sound sorry. "All children misbehave. It's my job...*our* job...to help them learn from their mistakes."

He knew perfectly well what his job was and he also knew that she didn't think he was very good at it, but this was neither the time nor the place to have that conversation. "I guess we should get started."

"I guess we should." She picked up the carrier and then smiled, which got the muscles in his chest to relax again. "I'll take him upstairs and be right down."

He stepped back to give her access to the stairs. "Oh. Sure. I'll grab a couple of boxes from your van."

"Thanks." She breezed past him, and there was that faint

hint of citrus again. "Oh. You'll need these." She handed him a set of keys.

He held out his hand and he'd swear he felt the tips of her fingers graze his palm.

Her clothing was a little more subdued than she'd been wearing at school the other day. She had on a narrow-fitting pair of jeans with the bottoms turned up into cuffs and an unbuttoned orange shirt with the sleeves rolled up partway. Under the shirt she wore a hot-pink T-shirt. Okay, not so subdued, but at least there was lots of coverage.

As he approached the passenger door of her van he could see a fire-safety booklet on the seat—the one with his phone number on it. He didn't know why it seemed significant that it was here, but it did. He unlocked the side doors and, as they swung open, a large wicker basket filled with clothing toppled toward him. He grabbed it before it hit the sidewalk, and another waft of her delicate perfume momentarily overtook him. He set the basket on the front steps and went back for some of the boxes.

He was staggering up the stairs with an armload of them, wishing he'd left one for the next trip, when he encountered Rory on her way down. She'd taken off the shirt, and the bright pink T-shirt turned out to be more of a tank top. Not so much coverage after all.

To give him enough room to get past, she flattened her back against the wall, causing her breasts to jut out a little. When they were at eye level, he couldn't help looking.

He climbed the rest of the stairs with the image of their perfect shape in his mind. He should not have looked. It was one thing to admire her feet, but the rest of her had to be strictly off-limits, especially now that they'd be living under the same roof.

The thought made him groan as he shouldered open the door to the apartment. He lowered the boxes to the floor and noticed a pair of green eyes gazing suspiciously at him from inside the pet carrier.

On his way back down the stairs he encountered Rory on her way up with the basket of clothing. This time it was his turn to make room for her. As she passed, her smile and the feel of her arm grazing his chest did some more crazy things to his insides. A few more run-ins like this and he'd be in danger of embarrassing himself.

"Why don't you stay up there and start unpacking? Let me carry everything upstairs."

She stopped and looked at him. "You don't mind?"

She was slightly winded from all the stairs, and the rise and fall of her chest made her breasts even more noticeable. Then she climbed another step to meet him at eye level, and he had the makings of an erection. "Don't mind at all."

She smiled back at him. "Thanks."

He watched the side-to-side sway of her curvy little rear end making its way up the stairs and reprimanded himself again. Watching her was not a good idea. Hell, none of this was a good idea.

He clumped down the stairs two at a time and was hauling a stack of canvases and another huge wicker basket full of shoes out of the van when he caught sight of his mother making her way up the street.

"Looks like our new tenant has arrived," she said.

He looked at her over the top of his load. "She has. Did you know she's Miranda's teacher?" He would really be ticked if she'd known about this and hadn't mentioned it.

"Rory is Miss Sunshine? I had no idea! Isn't that a surprise?"

That seemed to be the consensus, but he found it hard to believe she didn't know who Rory was.

"Is something bothering you?" she asked.

"No. It just seems odd that she turned out to be someone

we already know. And how is it that on the days you walk to and from school with Miranda, you've never met her?"

She seemed unfazed by the question. "We go as far as the corner and I wait there while she walks the rest of the way herself. What's the problem with that?"

Much as he'd like to, he couldn't think of one.

"At least you don't need to worry about what kind of influence she'll be on Miranda."

Right. Except now he wasn't worried about Miranda.

His mother dragged a box out of the van. "I'll run up and say hello."

"You don't have to carry this stuff. I can manage."

She gave him a sharp glance. "Cut the hero routine. It won't kill me to carry a few boxes."

Here we go, he thought. "I just meant—"

Betsy laughed and gave him a patronizing pat on the shoulder. "That womenfolk shouldn't be doing a man's work?"

Why do I even bother? he wondered. He followed his mother up the front steps, and Miranda met them at the door. "I'm ready to help. Should I bring something out of the van?"

"I thought you wanted to see the cat," Mitch said. The boxes he was holding were getting heavier by the second and he didn't want to leave Miranda out on the sidewalk by herself.

"Right!" She scampered up the stairs ahead of them. "Wait'll you see him, Grams! He's black and white and his name is Buick."

"What a great name."

As opposed to Dodge or Ford, Mitch thought, *which would be just plain silly.*

They trooped into the apartment, single-file.

Rory had already opened several boxes and seemed to

be studying their contents. "Betsy! Hi!" she said when she looked up.

"Where would you like these?" Mitch asked.

"Oh, anywhere."

"Need some help?" his mother asked.

"If you don't mind, I would really love that. Mitch already offered to carry everything upstairs for me."

"Did he now?" No one else would have detected the subtle reprimand in her voice, but it was there.

Mitch sighed. His mother could think whatever she liked, but he wasn't doing all this heavy lifting out of some misguided sense of chivalry. He was doing it because...

Rory chose that moment to bend over a box on the floor, providing him with a full-on view of the valley between her breasts. *That* was why he needed to spend as little time up here as possible. When he'd been married to Laura, he'd never looked twice at another woman. Now, his attraction to Rory felt wrong. Disloyal.

His mother tracked his gaze and smiled.

Damn. He quickly crossed the room and piled the boxes in an out-of-the-way corner. When he stood up, he banged his head on the sloped ceiling.

Everyone laughed.

He hotfooted it out the door and down the stairs, thinking, *This is the thanks I get?*

RORY SURVEYED THE ever-increasing pile of boxes and baskets full of her belongings. Mitch Donovan was doing almost too good a job of emptying out her van, and she was having trouble keeping up. Instead of asking her where she wanted things, he was stacking most of the boxes just inside the door. Other than his remark about her phone call earlier in the week, he didn't seem to want to talk much.

Miranda was sprawled on the floor with Buick, who had

ventured out of his carrier but not much farther. "Can you hear how loud he's purring?" Miranda asked.

"I sure can." Rory smiled at the little girl, once again regretting that she hadn't made time to look at Miranda's file. Given that Mitch and his daughter lived here with his mother, it seemed unlikely there was a wife in the picture. It wasn't common for a father to have custody, but it wasn't unheard-of. Or maybe Miranda was only here part of the time?

"Is there something I can do to help?" Betsy asked after checking the fridge and stove to make sure they'd been cleaned properly.

Rory hefted a box labeled Dishes onto the table and tore it open. "This is kitchen stuff. Would you mind unpacking it for me?"

"Happy to."

"Great," Rory said, feeling a little less overwhelmed. "I can't wait to have everything organized."

Betsy unwrapped a set of blue-glazed pottery dinner plates and set them on an open shelf above the counter. "Do you do a lot of entertaining?" she asked.

"Not really. I'm usually too busy during the school year and I like to travel during the summer vacation." Was she worried about too much noise? "I won't be having any wild parties up here."

"I didn't think you would." Betsy folded the newspaper she'd taken off the plates. "What about a boyfriend?"

Mitch appeared in the doorway, added two more boxes to the pile, and hesitated as though waiting to hear her reply.

"Oh…ah…no, actually…" The question caught her off guard, and knowing Mitch was listening made her feel strangely self-conscious. "I just moved to San Francisco so, um, I haven't had a chance to meet anyone."

Betsy smiled as she hoisted another box onto the table. "I'm sure that won't last. What do you think, Mitch? A beautiful woman like Rory won't be single for long."

He looked as if he'd rather fling himself down the stairs than answer that question. "There are only a few things left in the van. I'll just run down and grab them." From the thud of his footsteps, it sounded as if he took the stairs two at a time.

Betsy was still smiling after he left. "This is beautiful pottery."

"My mother's neighbor made those dishes for me when I went away to college. I've always loved them."

Betsy turned the plate over and examined the potter's mark. "I'm a potter, too, but I don't make tableware."

"What kind of work do you do?"

"Clay dragons," Miranda volunteered.

"Like the one on your front steps? He's charming."

The compliment was genuine, and Betsy looked flattered. "I also make planters, birdbaths, that sort of thing. If you'd like some pots and a garden ornament for your balcony, I'll bring them up for you."

Rory had no intention of venturing onto the balcony. Her fear of heights might be irrational, but it was still very real. "Thanks." She winked at Miranda. "A dragon will be good company for Buick, don't you think?"

The little girl stroked the cat's thick black fur. "I'll keep Buick company, too. I think he likes me."

"I can see that."

Buick rolled onto his back and Miranda giggled.

Rory opened a box of books and started sliding them onto the shelves that lined one wall in the living room.

"Lots of books," Betsy said as she arranged the rest of the plates on the shelf. "Are those travel guides?"

"I love to travel. Every summer since I started teaching

I've picked a state and visited a national park." She held up an Arizona guidebook. "This year I went to the Grand Canyon. My father sends me a lot of books, too. This will be the first place I've lived that actually has enough space for all of them. These built-ins are great."

"Mitch's father built those, and pretty much everything else up here."

"He did a wonderful job," she said. "I'm looking forward to meeting him."

"I'm afraid that won't be possible. He died five years ago."

"Oh, I'm so sorry."

"So am I, but no one lived a fuller life than he did."

Mitch appeared in the doorway, carrying her thrift-store slipper chair with a pile of cushions on the seat.

"Grams has a boyfriend now," Miranda said. "His name's Thomas and he looks like Santa Claus."

Mitch set the chair next to the sofa with a loud thump, clearly a reaction to his daughter's reference to the boy-friend, since he'd been pretty unobtrusive until then.

Best to let it go, Rory decided. "Is that everything?" she asked.

"Seems to be." He fished her keys from the pocket of his jeans. She thought he might toss them to her but he didn't, so she watched him watch her walk across the room. She stopped in front of him, held out her hand and waited. He set the keys on her palm, the same way she'd given them to him earlier, and there was no mistaking the subtle touch of his fingers.

When she turned around, a smiling Betsy was busy ar-ranging cups and saucers in a glass-doored cabinet. "You have lovely things." She set an old hand-painted floral-patterned teapot on the shelf next to the cups.

"Thanks. I'm always on the lookout for a good bargain

and I love vintage furniture and china, so I do a lot of shopping in thrift stores and secondhand shops. That chair Mitch just brought up is my latest find." The rose-patterned upholstery was slightly faded, which made it even more charming.

"Need help with anything else?" Betsy asked.

Although she tried, she couldn't think of anything. Betsy was already finishing up with the kitchen, which left Rory's clothes and her mother's artwork.

"I'll want to hang my mother's paintings, but it'll take me a while to decide where they should go."

"I'm sure Mitch would be happy to help with that."

Call me crazy, but Betsy seems like she's doing a little matchmaking. Before Rory had a chance to say she could hang the paintings herself, Betsy brought up her mother's exhibit.

"We've been invited to the opening of Rory's mother's art exhibit in a couple of weeks. It'll be a great experience for Miranda, don't you think?" she asked her son.

His nod seemed reluctant, but Rory took it as an affirmative.

"That's great. I'll be sure to give you all the details."

Betsy put the last few utensils into a drawer and slid it shut. "That's it. These things might not be organized exactly the way you want them, but at least they're unpacked."

"No problem. Everything looks great." The dress fitting later that afternoon meant she had less time than she'd like to get settled, so she appreciated all the help.

Mitch glanced around the small apartment, as though he was looking for something. "Is there a smoke alarm up here?"

"This house is *filled* with smoke alarms." Betsy moved the cushions off the chair and sat down. "A few years ago he gave me a case of them for Christmas," she said to Rory in a stage whisper.

"Did you install one up here?" he asked.

"It's over there by the skylight."

"When was the last time you tested it?"

"If I said yesterday, would you trust me and not check it yourself?"

"Did you test it yesterday?"

Betsy shook her head.

Rory laughed at them. Although neither seemed to realize they answered one question with another, their conversation was threaded with affection and Rory found it engaging.

Mitch walked to the other end of the apartment, reached up and pushed a button on the smoke alarm. Nothing happened. He removed the unit and looked at it. "There's no battery."

"Really?" Betsy didn't seem surprised. "The last tenant must have taken it out."

Mitch shook his head. "I have some downstairs. I'll go get one."

Rory couldn't decide if he was really being helpful, or if he was just looking for a reason to stick around. Either way worked for her. She rolled a couple of suitcases over to the closet and went back for the baskets full of shoes and handbags that Mitch had left at the top of the stairs.

"Are you sure there isn't anything else I can help with?" Betsy asked.

Rory inspected the apartment. There were still plenty of things to do, but her landlady's help had made a huge difference. "Would you like to make some tea? I could use a break."

"Will do."

Betsy was filling the kettle when Mitch returned with

a battery for the smoke detector. After he reinstalled it, he pushed the button again and it let out a loud squawk.

"Yikes." Rory clamped her hands over her ears. "I won't sleep through that."

"That's the idea."

"Hey, you scared Buick," Miranda said. "I think he needs something to play with. Does he have any toys?"

"He has a catnip mouse, but it must be still packed."

The little girl bounced to her feet. "I have a ball in my room. I'll go get it." She raced out the door and down the stairs.

"Why is he called Buick?" Betsy asked, reaching for the teapot and a tin of green tea.

"When he was a kitten, my mother said his purring sounded just like an old Buick my dad used to have. Apparently I was conceived in the backseat of that car."

Mitch rolled his eyes, but Betsy laughed. "Lighten up, for heaven's sake," she said to him. "It's funny."

He was *so* not amused. In fact, Rory was beginning to wonder if he had a sense of humor at all.

Miranda dashed back into the apartment, ball in hand. She rolled it across the floor and was crestfallen by Buick's disinterest.

Mitch seemed to relax. "We should get out of here and let you get settled," he said.

And before I say something else inappropriate, Rory thought. "Your mom's making tea. You and Miranda are welcome to stay if you'd like."

"Please, can we stay, Dad? Please, please, please?"

"We should go," he said.

"No fair. I hardly ever get to have tea."

Rory unfurled two gowns from the top of the basket and hung them on a hook by the closet door.

Ignoring her father, Miranda crossed the room and ran

her hand longingly over the cotton-candy-pink chiffon one. "These are like princess dresses."

"Not exactly," Rory said. "They're bridesmaid dresses."

"You've been a bridesmaid two times?" The little girl was wide-eyed and clearly impressed. "I wish I could be a flower girl someday, if anybody I know ever gets married."

Mitch's face went a little red, and Rory could swear she saw him squirm. Miranda seemed to know better than to push the issue any further, but it pretty much confirmed Rory's suspicion that the little girl's mother was no longer in the picture.

"These would be so awesome for dress-up," Miranda said.

Mitch stepped in. "You can't expect Rory to—"

"I think it's a great idea," Rory said. "I'll never wear them again. Tell you what. You can come up and visit me sometime and we'll have tea and play dress-up. As long as it's okay with your dad," she added quickly.

Miranda's hopeful little face gazed up at her father, and she was rewarded with a tentative nod. "That'll be so much fun," she said, turning her attention to the emerald-green dress.

"Another friend of mine is getting married next month, so there'll soon be three dresses for you to try on."

Miranda's eyes widened appreciatively. "Three?"

"You know what they say about three times a bridesmaid," Betsy said, grinning.

"What do they say?" Miranda asked.

Rory had heard it all before. "Three times a bridesmaid, never a bride."

"What does that mean?" Miranda asked.

"It means women who are always someone else's brides-maid never get to be a bride themselves."

Miranda gave her grandmother a horrified look. "Does that mean Miss Sunshine won't ever be able to get married?"

Mitch shifted his weight from one foot to the other, looking as though the subject made him uncomfortable.

"It's just a superstition," Rory said, amused by Miranda's question.

"What's a superstition?"

"Hm, let's see. Have you ever heard anyone say that Friday the thirteenth is an unlucky day?"

The little girl nodded.

"Well, that's a superstition. That day is no more unlucky than any other day, but people like to say it is."

"I see," Miranda said thoughtfully. "So you *will* be able get married."

"Actually, your grandmother's right about me not getting married. I'm not the marrying kind, but that has nothing to do with all the times I've been a bridesmaid." Although if she ever did get married, all these weddings had given her a clear idea of what she *didn't* want to do. Starting with putting her four best friends in outrageous gowns.

"I never regretted not having a wedding," Betsy said.

"You eloped?" Rory asked.

"Mitch's father and I never got—"

Before Betsy could finish, she was interrupted by loud throat-clearing from the other side of the room. She smiled sweetly at her son. "Mitch's father and I were *together* for thirty-five years and I never regretted a second of it. A *wedding* couldn't have improved that."

"You're lucky. The bride and groom from this wedding…" Rory indicated the emerald-green satin dress. "They've already split up. My parents separated and got back together more times than I can remember, and their divorce was…well, let's just say it wasn't pretty." And then there was Dean—a guy she'd dated for nearly six months before discovering he was still married to the woman who'd shown up at Rory's door, brimming with accusations and a suitcase crammed full of her husband's clothing. It had only taken Rory a couple of seconds to realize she didn't want him any more than his wife did.

"That has always been the problem with *conventional* marriage," Betsy said. "Getting out is a lot harder than getting in."

Mitch cast a disparaging glance at the ceiling, but he didn't say anything.

Interesting. Betsy and Mitch's father hadn't made a trip down the aisle…they hadn't even made it to city hall…but they'd obviously had a real marriage in every sense of the word. Unlike her parents, her friend Paige, her scum of an ex-boyfriend or, it would seem, even Mitch and Miranda's mother.

"If you don't get married," Miranda said, "you won't be able to have kids."

Again, all the grown-ups in the room exchanged looks.

"That's okay," Rory said. "I have twenty-four children in my classroom. That's a lot of kids."

Miranda giggled. "We're not your *real* kids."

Rory hugged her. "But you're all just as special to me."

"Then I want to stay in your class forever."

Rory laughed at that. "Third grade is a whole year away. For now I think we should concentrate on having fun in second grade, okay?"

"It's very sweet that the kids call you Miss Sunshine," Betsy said. "How did they think of that?"

Eventually, her name always came up. "I have both of my parents' last names—Pennington-Borland—which is quite a mouthful for my students. Sunshine is my middle name, so I use that instead."

Mitch leaned against the doorframe and, for the first time that morning, looked mildly amused.

"Rory is your first name?" Betsy asked.

"Not quite. It's short for Sonora."

"After the town?"

"I'm afraid so. It's where my parents got married." The first time. "They've always called me Rory, though, and I think it suits me better."

"Mitch's father and I had always said that if we had a girl, we'd call her Joni. Since we had a boy, we settled on Mitchell."

That was *exactly* like something her parents would have done. "She's still one of my dad's favorite singers. We used to sing 'Clouds' in the car when we drove down the coast from Mendocino. I was fascinated by the idea of ice-cream castles in the air."

"It would be *so* fun to live in an ice-cream castle." Miranda turned away from the pink bridesmaid dress, eyes wide with excitement. "I have an idea. You should come to Fisherman's Wharf with us this afternoon. Me and Dad are going there for ice cream."

Tempting, but not a good idea for so many reasons. "That sounds like fun and I love ice cream, but I have plans this afternoon."

Miranda looked disappointed, but Mitch's relief was palpable. Did he really think she'd tag along on their family outing?

"What's your favorite kind of ice cream?" Miranda asked.

Rory tried to think of one she *didn't* like. "All of them," she said.

Miranda laughed with her. "Me and my dad always get the same thing. My mom used to say we have no imaginations, but then she died and we stopped going for ice cream."

Oh. God.

Rory had *not* seen that coming.

Chapter Four

The downtown bus was packed. Rory clung to the overhead handrail and did her best to ignore the rap music blaring from the earbuds of the young man standing next to her. She'd missed the bus she should have taken and now she was running late. Argh. She should have driven instead. On the plus side, the walk to the bus stop and the ride downtown gave her a chance to digest the bombshell Miranda had dropped.

Mitch's silent and preoccupied manner made so much more sense now, and the death of Miranda's mother likely explained why the little girl was so mature for her age. Mitch had whisked her away almost immediately after her inadvertent confession, but Betsy and Rory had ended up chatting over a pot of tea, which was why Rory was late and still wearing her moving clothes.

Betsy had volunteered a few details about her son's circumstances. His wife had gone to get Miranda from a birthday party, but she'd never made it. A drunk driver had crashed into her car and she'd died at the scene. Mitch had been supposed to pick Miranda up, but he hadn't been able to get away from the fire hall. Of course, he blamed himself.

That had been more than a year ago. Last month, he and Miranda had moved in with Betsy so she could look after her granddaughter when Mitch was at work overnight. She had half-jokingly said that having them in the house cramped her—and Thomas's—style. And Mitch hadn't wanted to return to his old neighborhood, so they were all still adjusting to the new arrangement.

How could anyone not *want to live here?*

Rory had always dreamed about moving back someday. Now she was teaching at the very school she would have attended if her parents had stayed, and living in their old neighborhood. Everything was exactly as she had hoped it would be, except she hadn't expected to be living in such close quarters with a man who intrigued her more than any man had in a long time. Mitch Donovan had a lot of baggage, though—more than she was prepared to deal with, that was for sure—and she needed to be careful, especially given her track record with married men.

He's not married now, she reminded herself.

He's a grieving widower, herself reminded her back.

Her memory served up an image of his hand, large and strong, resting gently and protectively on his daughter's shoulders. He had amazing hands, and she had thought about them far too often since he'd visited her classroom.

Stop thinking about his hands, she warned herself. *Think about all the reasons why you, Sonora Sunshine Pennington-Borland, are not getting serious about anyone, especially not the single dad downstairs. That would be way too complicated.* Not that it would ever be an issue. He'd been annoyed that she'd called him about Miranda's behavior at school, which was puzzling at the time and even more so now that she'd seen them together at home. He was a good father who wanted the best for his daughter, so why the resentment?

She reached out and rang the bell for the next stop. The back door opened and she was nearly trampled by two teenaged boys who shoved their way inside, looking for a free ride. On the sidewalk, she hitched her oversize tote bag onto her shoulder and headed toward the bridal shop a few blocks away.

"Three times a bridesmaid, never a bride" worked for her. Marriage was hard. Marriage didn't last. Married couples fought, they cheated on each other, and then they got divorced.

Like her loser ex-boyfriend Dean, and her friend Paige and especially her parents. They'd met here in San Francisco during the infamous summer of love and had been living in an arrested state of flower childhood ever since. They just hadn't spent most of that time living together. Copper Pennington was happily ensconced in the little house they'd bought in Mendocino years ago when her career as an up-and-coming artist was taking off and she'd landed her first big commission. Sam Borland led a pseudo-bohemian existence in an upscale loft on Manhattan's Lower East Side. His last novel had held its own near the top of various bestseller lists for months, and it looked as though the new one would do the same.

For years now, Rory's mother had been in a casual, on-again-off-again relationship with her neighbor—the man who'd made the pottery Betsy had admired. Her father's current girlfriend had apparently been hired to set up his upcoming book tour. Rory hadn't met this one, but then she hadn't met most of the women who came and went from his life. She adored her dad but usually only saw him once a year, and she was grateful that their precious yearly visits didn't include his girlfriend of the hour.

Compared to her parents', Rory's life was remarkably conventional. She'd gone to college and landed her first teaching job right after graduation. At the same time, she was the least conventional of all her friends. Unlike them, she had no desire to get married and raise a family. She had meant what she said to Miranda—she loved her students, and they were all the family she needed.

She dodged a young mother pushing a baby stroller and narrowly avoided a head-on collision with an elderly woman who had stopped to admire the gurgling infant.

Come on, people. It's a baby. You've seen a million of them. And this one had a viscous-looking glob of drool bubbling down its chin. Ugh.

I'll take seven-year-olds any day. She loved teaching second grade. Kids that age were bursting with curiosity and enthusiasm, and they made going to work every day a joy. After ten years, teaching second grade still didn't feel like a job.

Seven-year-olds could follow simple instructions without questioning every step along the way. They could tie their own shoes. They could articulate ideas, at least in a basic way, and they threw themselves wholeheartedly into every opportunity presented to them. And they didn't drool.

She especially loved watching them while they wrote in their journals. Younger children hadn't yet developed the skills to put thoughts on paper, while older kids would sit and stare at a blank page, hypercritical of every idea even before it was fully formed. Second graders put pencil to paper without hesitation. They were quick-witted, yet naive enough to take things at face value. And they weren't afraid to use words they couldn't spell.

Seven was the perfect age. At school, Miranda was exceptionally energetic and imaginative—exactly the kind of child Rory loved having in her classroom. At home with her family, she seemed quieter and more serious. More like a miniature adult than a normal kid. Not surprising, given what she and her dad had been through, but Rory still hated to see a child grow up too quickly.

Even adults needed to relax and have some fun once in a while, and Rory liked to think she was still good at letting her inner child come out to play. Rory's father often joked that the nut didn't fall far from the tree, the tree in this case being Rory's mother. Copper Pennington's lively high-spiritedness sharply contrasted and often conflicted with Sam Borland's more serious bookishness. There was really no denying it...Rory was very much like her mother.

But that didn't mean *she* wanted to be a mother. In spite of having a wonderful relationship with both her parents, she was never one-hundred-percent convinced they'd wanted to be parents, either. If it hadn't been for that one night in the backseat of the Buick...

Rory sidestepped a half-dozen giggling teenaged girls who seemed to think they had the sidewalk, maybe even the world, all to themselves. *Am I the only person in downtown San Francisco who's in a hurry?* Even though a dress fitting wasn't high on her list of priorities today, she loved to spend time with her friends. Still, it would have been good to hang around the house and finish unpacking. Maybe catch a glimpse of Mitch.

You're not going there. Too much baggage, remember?

Baggage aside, a girl could still look. And admire the view.

She pushed through the door of the bridal salon, thinking that with everything else she had going on, she was lucky that being a maid of honor had turned out to be such an easy job.

Nicola and the others were seated at the back of the shop in a half circle of chairs facing a round dais and several full-length mirrors. The bride-to-be jumped up, brandishing her BlackBerry.

"There you are! I was just about to call you. I was

starting to worry." But she didn't look worried. More like a force to be reckoned with. Her short, sleek, dark hair was perfect, as always, and her tan-colored linen pants, white silk shirt, slender gold bangles and metallic ballet flats were as understated as they were expensive.

"Sorry I'm late. Since we're going out for drinks I left my van at home and took the bus."

The bride-to-be gave her a quick hug. "You should have called. I would have sent Jonathan to pick you up."

"I completely lost track of time. I would have called after I was on the bus but I left my cell phone at home." She waggled her fingers at Paige and Maria. "Hi, girls."

"Did you get moved into your new place?" Paige asked, squinting as she cleaned her glasses with the hem of her bulky gray sweater.

"I did, and it's perfect. My new landlady and her…her family helped me haul everything upstairs. They even helped me unpack, which is why I got sidetracked."

"You look gorgeous, as always. I love those colors on you." Maria, the truly gorgeous one with the Mediterranean complexion and captivatingly brown eyes, patted her protruding belly. "I'd get up and give you a hug, but it's too much work."

"How are you feeling?" Rory asked.

"Great. Except for all the kicking going on in here."

Rory stared at her friend's abdomen and tried to imagine how it would feel to have another human being living inside her. Her imagination failed her.

A young woman stepped out from behind a rack of dresses. She was small-boned and lively, with a mass of shiny dark curls held off her face by a wide, red headband. "You must be the maid of honor," she said to Rory.

"She is," Nic said. "This is Rhoda, my seamstress."

"Have a seat with the other gals. Their dresses

have already been fitted. I'll bring out yours in a few minutes."

Rory dropped her bag on the floor and settled into a chair. When she stretched her legs and crossed her ankles, Nicola eyed her painted canvas sneakers. "Please tell me you remembered to bring shoes."

She reached down and patted her bag. "I brought a pair that might go with the dress, but once I've seen it I might look for something else."

"I knew I could count on you. Wish I could say the same for Jess."

"Jess doesn't own any dressy shoes. You know that," Paige said.

"Where is she?" Rory asked.

Nic nodded toward a curtained cubicle. "Jess? What's taking so long?"

A slit appeared in the curtain and Jess's head popped out, all flashing green eyes and fiery red hair. "Should I take off my bra or leave it on?"

Nicola exhaled a long-suffering sigh. "Leave it on. The dress won't fit properly without it."

"So it's okay that the straps are showing?"

The others laughed. Nic did not. "Can you slip the straps off your arms and tuck them inside the dress?"

"If I do that, I might as well take it off."

That brought on the bride's characteristic eye roll. "Oh, for heaven's sake. Leave it on and let us see the dress."

The curtain parted and Jess stepped out. The hem of the blue dress dragged on the floor, a pair of dingy white bra straps emerged above the top, and her arms were tightly crossed under her breasts. "I need help with the zipper."

The seamstress quickly came forward and zipped the dress. "Stand up here and let's have a look at you."

Jess climbed onto the dais, revealing a pair of battered

black-and-white high-topped sneakers. She still hadn't unfolded her arms.

Rory grinned at Nicola. "I see what you mean about the shoes."

"That's our girl. A total disaster and still so darned lovable. I'm counting on you to help her find a pair of shoes and some decent lingerie."

"Why me?" Shopping with Jess was as much fun as a trip to the dentist. Or the gynecologist. Or both. On the same day.

Nic's eyes sparkled. "You're my maid of honor. It's part of your job."

A job that suddenly didn't seem so easy after all. "You're evil."

"*Hello?*" Jess said. "I'm standing right here. It's not like I can't hear you."

Nic ignored her. "She and Maria would end up arguing, and she'd run roughshod over Paige. You're good at getting people to do things. It's what makes you such a great teacher."

All true, Rory thought, even as she acknowledged Nicola's blatant use of flattery to get what she wanted. But shopping with Jess? The girl's wardrobe consisted of jeans, T-shirts, the men's dress shirts she wore with the sleeves rolled up to the elbows, and lingerie that may very well have been purchased in the previous millennium.

Still, Nicola's affectionate comment about Jess being lovable was so true. She was fiercely independent and generous to a fault. She'd struggled her whole life to make ends meet, and yet she'd give you one of those godawful shirts right off her back. She could also be painfully honest, and this was one of those times.

"No offense, but you could have picked dresses that had sleeves and weren't so poofy."

Instead of being offended, Nicola laughed. "None taken, and I've already told you, we need a dress that can be altered to fit Maria, and this one is perfect for her."

Once again Maria ran her hands over her enormous belly. "Don't blame me," she said. "This is all the fault of my darling husband. Tony weighed just over ten pounds when he was born, and he was the smallest of his three brothers."

"You have a ten-pound baby in there?" Jess asked.

"Note to self. Check birth weight of prospective husbands." Paige gazed longingly at Maria's baby bump. "So you know it's a boy?"

"No, we don't want to know ahead of time. As long as it's healthy, we don't care if it's a boy or girl." Maria gave them a sly smile. "But I'm secretly hoping it's a girl. And Tony not-so-secretly would like a boy."

Paige had desperately wanted to start a family since the day she got married—even before that, actually. Her husband had insisted they wait, and it was a good thing they had because he'd moved out a couple of months ago.

"I'm sure you and Dan will work everything out," Maria said.

Paige shook her head. "I don't think so."

Poor Paige. Rory could tell she was trying to be stoic, but anyone could see she was hurting. "Have you talked to him lately?"

"He called last week to tell me he wants a divorce. He thought he should let me know so I could talk to a lawyer."

The jerk, Rory thought, but she kept it to herself.

Jess was less subtle. She made a fist and punched her other palm with it. "You want me to have a talk with him?" Her dress shifted a little and she quickly crossed her arms again.

"You should talk to Nicola," Maria said.

"She already has," Nic assured them. "I've set her up with an excellent lawyer in our firm. Suffice to say, Danny Boy won't know what hit him."

Jess was undeterred. "I'll still be glad to have a little chat with him."

Paige laughed. "Thanks…I think…but there's no need. Everything is under control." For a woman who'd wanted to get married and start a family more than anything else in the world, Paige seemed awfully matter-of-fact about the end of a marriage that had lasted less than two years.

Rhoda politely but firmly cut into their conversation. "Ladies, I can't fit this dress unless this one holds still. Now, arms down at your sides please."

Jess slowly lowered her arms. She looked as though she expected the dress to slither down her slender body, but it stayed where it was.

"I'd like Jess to stay in her dress so I can see her and Rory together. I'd like to figure out how we should do your hair."

"Good idea." Rhoda brought out Rory's dress and hung it in the fitting room.

Rory carried her tote bag into the cubicle, quickly undressed and shimmied into the dress. She sat on a softly padded chair, blue taffeta rustling around her as she buckled the narrow straps of her shoes.

"Will you be wearing heels?" Rhoda was asking Jess as Rory stepped out of the dressing room.

Nicola shot Jess a pointed look. "Yes, she will."

The seamstress knelt on the edge of the dais and measured the excess hem. "Very good. If you wear at least a three-inch heel, we won't have to shorten the dress."

Jess's eyebrows reacted, but before she could object, Rhoda stood and shifted her attention to the top of the dress.

"Now this is a different matter. You'll need a strapless bra, and maybe some gel inserts would help—"

"Excuse me?" Jess looked as though she'd like to strangle the woman with her own measuring tape.

Rory drew her lips between her teeth and pressed them together to stop the grin. Jess didn't need any encouragement.

Paige gazed across the store as though something had just caught her attention.

Maria looked down at her belly.

Nicola was staring straight at Jess's bustline. Or lack thereof. "That's actually a good idea."

"They'll give the dress some shape. I'll show you." Rhoda disappeared into an office and emerged half a minute later with two pale pink imitation breasts, one in each hand. "They're comfortable and natural-looking—"

"And they are *not* getting stuffed in here," Jess said, using her two index fingers to indicate where the fake breasts weren't going.

Maria's dark eyes sparkled. "A little extra boobage can't hurt."

Jess glared at her.

Rory finally gave in and laughed out loud. The seamstress looked disappointed, but she handed the inserts to Nicola and slid her measuring tape off her neck. "All right, then. Arms up and out to the side so I can take this measurement."

Jess complied, then craned her neck in an attempt to see what the woman was writing on her clipboard.

Rory's 34B seemed to do the job quite nicely. She didn't know what Jess's bra size was, and until now she hadn't known her friend was so sensitive about it. Jess had always been the tomboy of the group, and the oversize men's dress shirts she usually wore did an admirable job of hiding her modest assets.

"This blue is perfect for you blondes and redheads," the seamstress said. Rory wasn't sure anyone else would agree. What Nic had described as periwinkle had turned out to be a startlingly bright electric blue, and the shiny taffeta fabric seemed to grab every particle of light in the room and reflect it back at ten times its original amplitude. *If light rays had amplitude,* she thought absently. Whatever they had, these were the bluest dresses she had ever seen.

And Jess had been right about the poofiness, an effect created by big tucks and gathers that Rhoda referred to as ruching. Rory didn't know what Nicola saw when she looked at these dresses—maybe in her soon-to-be-wedded bliss she was seeing them through rose-colored glasses— but Rory knew someone who would fall completely in love with hers.

Miranda. After this wedding, they would have three dress-up options.

While the seamstress took measurements and marked the dress where alterations were needed, Rory's mind drifted back over the things Betsy had said. Mitch's marriage had been very traditional, and his wife had been a full-time mom. Had she played dress-up with their daughter?

"Rory?" Nicola asked.

"Hm?"

"I was agreeing that this is a great color for the two of you."

"Sorry. I must've been daydreaming."

"Now that I see the two of you in your dresses, I think you should both wear your hair down. Do you mind?" she asked, reaching for Jess's ponytail.

Jess made a face but otherwise didn't object. She never wore her hair down, but since this would be Nic's day, she could call the shots. "We can pull your hair back off your face, like this," she said, demonstrating what she had in mind, "and have a cascade of curls down your back. Maria? Paige? What do you think?"

"They're tall and thin and gorgeous," Maria said. "Like a pair of supermodels."

Paige took off her glasses and wiped them with the bottom edge of her sweater. "I think I should have tried to lose weight before the wedding."

"Nonsense," Maria said. "You're gorgeous, too. All soft curves and voluptuous. Lots of men love that. I will admit, though, that when I was a teenager, I would have given just about anything to look like these two. Now all I want is a waistline."

"I've never seen a more radiant mother-to-be," Paige said. "In a few months you'll have a waistline *and* a beautiful baby. If it's a girl, she'll be a raven-haired beauty like her mom."

"Your time will come," Maria assured her.

Paige pouted. "Not at the rate I'm going."

"After the baby's born, I'll let you babysit. You can invite Dan over to talk, he'll take one look at you with a baby in your arms, and he'll change his mind."

Seriously? Rory thought looking after a baby might be the best birth control ever invented.

The seamstress knelt to check the length of Rory's dress. "Are these the shoes you'll be wearing?" she asked.

"These or something similar." Since she had to take Jess shoe-shopping, she might as well look for a new pair, too.

Nicola lifted the edge of the voluminous skirt and studied Rory's silver high-heeled sandals. "They're perfect. I hope Jess can find a pair like these."

"I can't walk in heels like that!"

"Jess, you're one of my best friends and you know I love you, but you're *not* wearing sneakers to my wedding."

"What if I buy new ones?" Jess asked. "Blue ones?"

Nicola laughed at the joke, but Rory suspected Jess was only half kidding. "Rory has already agreed to take you shoe-shopping. Unless you'd rather go with me."

Jess's eyes widened in mock horror. "No!" Grinning, she hitched up the hem of her dress, uncovered one sneaker, and planted her foot next to Rory's. "Our tastes are so similar."

Typical Jess. She loved having the last word as much as Nic liked having her own way. In spite of their different interests and upbringings, the five of them had become friends when they were dorm mates in their first year at college. Nic and Maria were from affluent San Franciscan families, and they were carrying on the tradition by "marrying well." Paige's military family had moved all over the country and now she was determined to put down roots and raise a family. Jess had been raised by her mom and her grandfather. She'd never met her father and by all reports, that was not a bad thing. Rory's parents' on-again-off-again marriage hadn't provided the most stable environment, either, but she'd had it a lot easier than Jess.

Maria had been the first to get married, and they had agreed then that each would have a turn at being maid of honor. Paige had been Maria's and Nicola had been Paige's. Maria would be Jess's and, if Rory was ever crazy enough to tie the knot, she'd have Jess.

"You can wear sneakers at my wedding," Rory said to her.

"You said you're never getting married."

Rory grinned. "That's why I'm letting you wear sneakers."

"When you change your mind, don't think I won't hold you told to it. I have witnesses."

The seamstress stood and draped her measuring tape around her neck. "That's it, ladies. I'll need each of you to come in for a final fitting, especially the mother-to-be. I've allowed for a little expansion, but we want a perfect fit."

A faint pink glow softened Maria's olive-toned skin. "That's very sweet of you, but what about Nicola's dress? Don't we get to see it?"

Nic exchanged a sly glance with Rhoda. "Not a chance. I'm keeping it completely under wraps until my big day. Now let's head to The Whiskey Sour for some girl talk. Drinks are on me."

Chapter Five

Fisherman's Wharf teemed with Saturday afternoon visitors. Mostly tourists, if Mitch had to guess. Gulls circled and squawked overhead, their raucousness punctuated by honking taxi cabs and the occasional ship's whistle.

Miranda tugged at his hand, urging him to hurry. Her favorite ice-cream place was still a couple of blocks away, and Mitch knew that after they'd fulfilled that expectation she would slow down and spend some time looking at the boats and the markets and the souvenir stalls.

In the old days, he used to carry her on his shoulders and Laura would slip her hand into his. He was glad his daughter hadn't suggested riding on his shoulders today because he wasn't sure he could handle having that hand empty.

It's one afternoon, he reminded himself. *If Miranda can do this, so can you.* Besides, being here felt oddly...right. Even though it was just the two of them, this was easier than he'd expected it to be.

"I'm glad Miss Sunshine moved in with us, aren't you?" his daughter asked.

Truthfully, he would need a little time to process that unexpected turn of events. "She isn't living *with* us," he said. "She's renting the apartment upstairs." It was as much a reminder for himself as it was for his daughter. Rory had her own apartment, her own life, and she was free to come and go without him and his family keeping tabs on her every move.

"I know, but she said I could visit her and Buick whenever I want. The kids at school are going to be sooo jealous."

That was probably true. From what he'd seen, the other students were as crazy about Miss Sunshine as Miranda was. "It was nice of her to say you can visit, but you always need to check with me or Grams first."

"Why?" Her blond curls bobbed in the breeze as she rotated her head to look up at him.

"We've been over this, Miranda. You're not old enough to leave the house on your own."

A cable car clanged in the distance. If the sound registered with Miranda, she didn't let on. "But Miss Sunshine's apartment is *inside* our house."

"That part of the house is hers now."

"Why?"

These days, *why* was her favorite word. "Because she pays for it. That makes it hers."

"But she said I could."

Mitch gently squeezed her hand and looked down at her, making every effort to smile. "I know she did, but Grams and I will be worried if we can't find you, and we might not think to look for you in Rory's apartment."

She seemed to process that information as she hopped along on one foot. "Okay, I'll ask first. But you have to say yes 'cause she said I could go anytime I want."

Mitch sighed. "Thank you for saying you'll ask first." He wanted to explain that just because she wanted to do something didn't mean the answer would always be yes, but he stopped himself. This afternoon was about having fun, about the two of them managing to be a family on their own.

The hopping stopped and she resumed walking. "Rory's a cool name, isn't it?"

"Yes, but it's just a nickname."

"What's that?"

One of these days he'd learn to agree with her rather than give out information that resulted in a never-ending stream of questions. "Sometimes a nickname is a short version of a person's real name."

"Like your name is really Mitchell instead of Mitch?"

"Right. Or it can be a different name, like Grams's. Her real name is Elizabeth, but everyone calls her Betsy."

"I wonder what Miss Sunshine's real name is."

He knew it was Sonora, but if he told Miranda, would she tell the other kids in her class? Probably, and it wasn't like Miss Sunshine didn't have enough names already. "I don't know," he said to Miranda, hoping they could stop talking about her teacher.

"She's lucky she's got a cat. Can we get one?"

"No," he said.

Miranda's head swiveled sharply and she gave him a surprised look. "Don't you like cats?"

"No. I mean, yes. Cats are fine, but I don't think it's a good idea to have one when you're at school all day and I'm at work. Besides, I don't think Grams wants a cat."

"She likes Buick."

She had that right. His mother seemed completely infatuated with the new tenant, cat and all.

Laura had been allergic to cats. Within minutes of being around one, she'd start to sneeze and her eyes would go red and puffy, so having one had been out of the question. It seemed Miranda hadn't inherited that problem.

"Here we are," he said, relieved to switch the conversation from Rory's cat to ice cream. The subject was sure to come up again, and when it did, he hoped to have a better reason not to get one.

Miranda looked up at the long list of ice-cream flavors posted next to the window. "If Mom was here, what kind do you think she'd order?"

Mitch waited for his grief to stab him in the chest, but it didn't happen. So he scanned the list and picked one. "She liked peaches and cream."

"That's what I was going to say!" She tipped her head back and smiled up at him. "But I'm having chocolate-chip cookie dough."

Mitch ordered the ice cream for his daughter and watched the young man skillfully pile two scoops onto the cone.

"And for you, sir?" he asked, carefully passing the cone across the counter to Miranda.

For a split second, he thought about ordering Laura's likely choice, then decided he was being sentimental. Besides, he didn't like peaches and cream.

"Chocolate."

Miranda slid her mouth across the top scoop and came away with an ice-cream moustache. "I knew you'd say that. I like it when things stay the same."

So did he.

He handed her a napkin, wishing he could shake the feeling that their lives weren't finished changing.

THE WHISKEY SOUR was next to empty when they arrived. Eric, Jess's part-time bartender, was sharing a laugh with two middle-aged men seated at the bar. Rory had seen them there before. They were mechanics who worked in the neighborhood, regular patrons from the days when Jess's grandfather had run the place.

The upscale improvements in the South of Market neighborhood hadn't extended to The Whiskey Sour. To everyone's disbelief, Jess had walked away from a teaching career to take over the bar after her grandfather passed away. She had two reasons for not making any changes—an overabundance of sentimentality for the man who had practically raised her and a complete lack of financial resources. Now surrounded by funky delis and eateries and trendy loft condos, The Whiskey Sour was a bit of a blast from the past.

It wasn't the kind of place Rory and her friends would normally frequent, but she appreciated its unpretentiousness and the fact that they were often the only patrons. This was good for them, but not so good for Jess. Rory worried about her, but she insisted she earned enough to keep herself alive and the bar in business.

Eric gave his jaw-length sandy-blond hair a girlish toss and waved at them from behind the bar. "Hey, pretty ladies. I've been expecting you."

Jess joined him. "I can't believe you're flirting with my friends."

"How do you know I wasn't flirting with you?" he asked.

"Because you know better."

Paige, Maria and Nicola settled into their usual table in the corner by the front window. Rory leaned on the bar and winked at Eric. "If you think she's pretty now, wait'll you see her in strapless blue taffeta."

He draped a brotherly arm around his boss's shoulder and closed his eyes. "I can just picture it." He opened them again. "Did you know she's already asked me to be her wedding planner when she gets married?"

Eric loved to tease Jess, and he was one of the few people who got away with it. Their grandfathers had been lifelong friends, and Jess and Eric had grown up together. He'd been there through her tumultuous teenage years, and she'd been his confidante while he'd figured out why he never seemed to fit in.

Jess ducked out from under his arm and reached for a couple of glasses. "When I get married, there might be a justice of the peace but no way will there be a wedding planner."

Eric cupped a hand to his mouth and leaned over to Rory. "She's right, poor darling," he said to her in a stage whisper. "Any man willing to marry a woman who dresses like a lumberjack won't expect a real wedding. Just a kegger and a bucket of take-out chicken."

Jess hoisted her nose in the air, pretending to be offended.

"Go." He took the glasses from her. "Sit with your friends and I'll bring your drinks over. I assume everyone wants the usual."

"Coffee for me, but I can get it."

He set the glasses on the counter and gave her an affectionate shove toward the corner table. "Go. I'm not exactly rushed off my feet."

"Whatever's in the pot will do."

After Eric arrived with a tray of drinks, Rory raised her glass and the others joined her. "Here's to weddings, babies, new beginnings and old friends."

Jess added a splash of cream to her cup and gave it a stir. "Hear, hear," she said. She took a sip from her mug and made a face. "I should have had him put a shot of whiskey in this."

The cream had turned the coffee a revolting shade of gray. "When was that made?" Rory asked.

"I don't know. Lunchtime?"

"Ew!"

"That's disgusting!"

"That's sewer sludge, not coffee," Nicola said. "Why don't you make a fresh pot?"

Because Jess's cash flow was barely a trickle.

"I would if a customer was drinking it." She laughed off the collective groans and grimaces, set the mug on the table and cracked her knuckles. "So, who besides me doesn't have a date for Nic's wedding?"

Nicola rolled her eyes. "What about you, Rory?"

"I haven't been in the city long enough to find a date." Just long enough to meet someone who was so wrong for her in so many ways. "Maybe I'll ask Eric."

"You're out of luck. Eric's covering the bar that night so I can be at the wedding."

Too bad. Eric would be the perfect no-strings-attached date.

"No one's asked if *I* have a date," Paige said.

Newly separated, shy and—let's face it—somewhat insecure, Paige had a date for the wedding?

"Dan left two months ago and you're already seeing someone? Go, Paige," Rory said.

"Not technically, but remember my old college friend Andy? Well, for the past couple of weeks we've been getting together for coffee. I asked him to go with me and he said yes."

"I thought he had a girlfriend," Jess said.

"They broke up around the same time Dan moved out. I don't know how I'd have managed this without Andy."

Maria struggled to sit up straight. "Are you saying we haven't been supportive?"

"You guys have been great, but misery loves company and since Andy and I have been going through the same thing, we've been each other's shoulder to cry on."

"Didn't Andy used to have a thing for you?" Jess asked.

Paige shook her head vigorously. "No way. I'm not his type."

Everyone looked at everyone else. "Right," Jess said. "He's probably not interested in smart, beautiful women."

Paige fidgeted with her glasses. "I'm an overweight librarian. Andy's a fitness freak and a total daredevil."

"You are *not* overweight!" Maria said. "And anyway, what does that have to do with anything?"

"Um, everything? Can you believe he invited me to go white-water rafting?"

"You should go," Rory said. "It's so much fun!"

Jess set her half-empty mug on the table and pushed it away. "I forgot about your Grand Canyon rafting trip. How was it?"

"I loved it. Best summer vacation yet."

"It must have been freaky, having all that rock towering over you."

"I'm not claustrophobic," she reminded them. "Just terrified of heights."

Paige seemed relieved that the conversation had shifted away from her. "What was it like to stand on the edge and look into the canyon?"

"I wouldn't know."

"Seriously? You didn't go to the rim?" Nic asked.

"Totally serious. Besides, everyone does that, but hardly anyone does the raft trip."

"Where are you going next year?"

"I'm not sure, but I'm thinking one of the national parks on the east coast."

"Rory!" Paige peered over the top of her glasses. "You *can't* drive across the country in that ancient old van."

"Vanna White's running very well these days, thank you. But getting back to white-water rafting—"

"Do it," Jess said. "You'll have a blast."

"And you'll have Andy to hold on to," Nicola said. "What's more fun than that?"

"You're all insane," Paige said. "Andy and I are just friends, and that's not going to change." She sipped her wine. "Rory, you haven't told us about your new place."

"I can't wait for you guys to see it. It's an attic apartment in one of those big old Victorians just off Haight Street and only a couple of blocks from the school. My landlord's the neatest woman, a lot like my parents."

"An old hippie?" Maria asked.

Everyone laughed.

"So it's just the two of you?" Nic asked.

"That's what I thought at first, but her son and his daughter live there, too."

"What's he like?"

"How old is he?"

"How old is the daughter?"

"No wife?"

Rory laughed. She should have know that would cause a stir. "Slow down."

"We need details," Maria said.

How much to tell them? "I'm guessing mid-thirties. His daughter, Miranda, is seven, and she's in my class."

"And Miranda's mother?" Nic asked.

"I just found out this morning that she died in a car accident. Isn't that awful?"

"What about her father?" Paige asked. "Where does he work?"

"San Francisco Fire Department. He's a—"

"A *firefighter?*" they chorused.

"I think I know who he is," Nic said. "Is he hot?"

Rory's face suddenly was.

Jess laughed and jabbed her with an elbow. "Rory thinks so."

"Jonathan plays basketball with a couple of firefighters. Some kind of fun social league. I remember him saying a year or so ago that one of the guys lost his wife. What's his name?"

Rory was reluctant to say, but her friend would find out one way or another. "Mitch Donovan."

Nic took out her BlackBerry. "I'll text Jonathan and see what I can find out."

"No!" Rory grabbed her wrist. "He might get the wrong idea."

"I'll be subtle." Nicola's thumbs worked in frenetic tandem. "There we go." She sent the message and set the device on the table in front of her.

Rory sighed. "What if he tells Mitch we're gossiping about him?"

"Guys never talk about stuff like that."

"That poor little girl," Paige said. "Growing up without a mother."

"I can't imagine." Maria ran a protective hand over her belly. "If her mother was anything like me, she was already thinking ahead to her daughter's first date, high-school graduation…"

"Okay," Jess said, "that's depressing. Can we talk about something else?"

Nicola grinned. "Like Rory living under the same roof as a deliciously good-looking firefighter. You should ask him to come to the wedding with you."

"No! And how do you know what he looks like?"

"I've seen the guys on the team. If he's the one I think he is, he is beyond delicious."

That would be Mitch. "I'm not inviting him to the wedding. His daughter is one of my students, we live in the same house. That would be way too complicated, and I don't do complicated."

"Love doesn't have to be complicated," Maria said.

"Who said anything about love? I just met him!"

"One of these days you'll fall head over heels for someone, and you'll see it's the simplest thing in the world."

"For a widower with a seven-year-old? I don't think so."

Nicola's BlackBerry buzzed. She picked it up and smiled triumphantly. "I was right. Mitch Donovan *is* on Jonathan's basketball team. Too bad we didn't invite those guys to the wedding."

If Rory wanted Mitch to remain uninvited, she knew the best thing to do was to say nothing.

Nicola tucked her BlackBerry into her handbag. "And while I'm on the subject of weddings, we haven't talked about my bridal shower."

"I thought that was supposed to be a surprise," Rory said.

"Don't you dare surprise me. I do not want to show up for my shower in old blue jeans and no makeup."

Like that could ever happen.

"That's what you guys did to me." Paige looked accusingly at Maria.

"I've apologized for that a dozen times," Maria said. "What else can I say? It seemed like a good idea."

"If you don't want to be surprised, Nic, you'd better send me your schedule for the next couple of weeks," Rory said. "We plan to have it here and Jess needs some advance notice—"

"Here? No way. Sorry, Jess," Nic added quickly. "It's a great place to hang out, but I *can't* have my shower in a… a bar."

Jess held up both hands. "No problem. I told her it was a bad idea."

Rory tried to imagine a bridal shower in her new apartment. "My place isn't big enough. Paige and Jess don't have enough room, either, and Maria lives too far out of the city."

"Call my mother. Here's her number in case you don't have it handy." Nic jotted it on a cocktail napkin. "Our house is perfect for this sort of thing."

Our house being her family's Cow Hollow mansion near the Presidio. Rory loved that house, especially its views of the bay, but she wondered if there might be another option. The only person in the world who was a bigger control freak than Nicola was Nicola's mother.

Jess gave them all a sly wink. "So your mother'll be okay with the male stripper?"

"You wouldn't dare."

"She just likes to bug you," Rory said.

The bride-to-be wasn't letting go that easily. "If you ever *do* get married, little Miss Sunshine, just remember who'll be your maid of honor."

"And I'll be fine with a surprise shower here at The Whiskey Sour."

Jess grinned.

"But no stripper."

They all laughed at that. Easy for them, she thought. And so much for the idea that being a maid of honor would be easy. She hadn't bargained on shoe-shopping with Jess or teaming up with Nic's mother to throw a shower.

Maria covered a yawn. "I have to get going. This has been so much fun, especially finding out that Paige has a new man in her life and Rory is living with a handsome firefighter. Anything else I should know before I leave?"

"I almost forgot. You're all invited to my mother's

opening." Rory took a handful of cards out of her bag and passed them around.

"I think we already have a commitment that night." Nicola scrolled through the calendar on her BlackBerry. "We do. Dinner with one of the senior partners at Jon's firm."

"Tony doesn't like me driving into the city alone at night, and I'll never be able to drag him into an art gallery."

"That's okay," Rory assured her. "The last thing we need is for you to go into labor on the bridge."

"I'm here on Wednesdays," Jess said.

"You don't have to look so relieved," Rory teased.

"No offense, but art's not my thing."

No kidding. Jess's idea of art was a Han Solo poster and a neon beer sign.

"Paige, what about you?"

"I love your mom's work and it would be great to see her again, but that's the night Andy and I get together after work."

"Sorry," they all said in unison.

"No problem." Just as well none of them were going, since Mitch and his daughter were.

"GOOD NIGHT, DADDY."

"Good night, princess," Mitch said from the doorway of his daughter's bedroom. "Want me to leave the hall light on for a while?"

Her head bobbed against the pillow. "Just till I fall asleep, 'kay?"

"You bet." He closed the door partway so the light wasn't shining directly on her face.

"Daddy?"

He leaned back into her room. "Yes?"

"Today was fun."

More fun than he'd expected. "We'll have to do it again soon," he said, bracing himself for the inevitable request that next time included a ride on a cable car.

"And Miss Sunshine can come with us, right?"

Okay, he had not seen *that* coming. It might take some time, but eventually he hoped Miranda would accept that although Miss Sunshine was living in their house, she wasn't part of their family. She had a life of her own and wouldn't expect or even want to be included in their activities. "We'll see," he said.

"Good," Miranda said. "Let's ask her tomorrow."

Do all kids do this? Hear one thing when they've been told something else? "We'll talk about it in the morning, okay?"

"'Kay. G'night."

"Good night," he said. "Sleep tight." Then he quickly slipped out of the room before she had time to ask any more questions about Rory.

He still couldn't believe that she, of all people, had moved into the attic apartment. He did not need the temptation of a beautiful woman living in the house, especially a woman who didn't altogether approve of the way he was raising his daughter.

Downstairs, he made two restless circuits of the living room. Miranda was right. They'd had fun this afternoon, and yet he couldn't shake the feeling that it had been a strange day. He felt as if things were changing again. He didn't like change and he was only just getting used to the way things were now.

He needed something to do, he thought, wandering into the kitchen. He and Miranda had helped his mother clean up after dinner, then Betsy had gone down to organize some stuff in her basement studio. He could hear her clattering around down there and it sounded as though she might be a while, which was fine because he wasn't sure he wanted company.

He poured himself a cup of cold coffee and stuck it in the microwave. After it pinged, he carried the mug into the living room. From the window he could see Rory's van parked on the street in front of the house. He and Miranda had arrived home late in the afternoon to find the van parked at the curb, right where she'd left it that morning. Miranda had begged to go upstairs to see her, but his mother said Rory had taken the bus downtown because she and her friends planned to go for drinks after the dress-fitting. She scored points for being responsible about not drinking and driving. If only everyone was, he thought bitterly.

Today, fourteen months after the accident that had robbed him and his daughter of the most important person in their lives, the afternoon at Fisherman's Wharf had been just what they needed. He'd been avoiding doing the things Laura loved, assuming it would be too painful—not just for him, but for Miranda, too. That hadn't been the case at all. Miranda had held his hand and talked nonstop about school and cats and Miss Sunshine. The only time she mentioned her mother had been at the ice-cream stand. She was happy with her memories of her mother. Instead of trying to avoid them, he owed it to his daughter to preserve them. He hadn't been doing that. If anything, he'd wanted to bury the memories along with his wife because it hurt too damned much to let them live.

So what had changed? Selling his place and moving back into his mother's house? Getting involved at Miranda's school? Meeting Rory?

He drained his mug and set it on the coffee table. A crash in the basement was followed by his mother's voice, no doubt using some colorful language. He contemplated going downstairs to see if she needed a hand, then thought better of it. He'd grown up with a mother who could bake bread, change a flat tire and rescue the neighbor's cat from a tree—and all before breakfast. If she needed help, she'd ask for it.

He put his feet up on the coffee table and leaned back against the sofa. He was tired from spending the day with his mother and daughter and the new tenant, but it was different from the way he felt after responding to a fire. This was mental exhaustion. Maybe a good night's sleep was what he needed. After he climbed the stairs, he looked in on Miranda, who was sleeping soundly, then went into his own room and shut the door. As he pulled his T-shirt over his head and tossed it into the laundry basket in the closet, he heard a car door slam in front of the house. He glanced around the edge of the curtain in time to see a taxi pulling away and Rory walking up the front walk. He quickly let the curtain drop, hoping she hadn't noticed.

The front door opened and closed, and he stood in the middle of his bedroom, stock-still, listening to her footsteps on the stairs. At the sound of her apartment door clicking closed, he gave his head a shake. He didn't need to pay attention to her comings and goings, but having another person in the house would take some getting used to.

He turned on his reading lamp before turning off the overhead light, stripped off the rest of his clothes and slid between the sheets. Then he reached for a magazine on the nightstand and flipped it open.

A floorboard creaked overhead. He couldn't hear her footsteps, but the ancient floor let him track her progress from one part of the apartment to another. And he wasn't sure, but he thought he could hear her voice. She'd definitely come home alone—was she talking to herself? No, probably to the cat.

He perused the magazine's table of contents, looking for a distraction. It was a parenting magazine he'd picked up at the grocery store the day he'd visited Miranda's classroom. Laura had always seemed to know what to do, how to handle their daughter, and he'd been more than happy to trust her judgment. Their arrangement had been a traditional one, about which his mother had periodically made disparaging comments, but it had worked for them. Now, as often as not, he felt at a loss. He knew he couldn't learn parenting skills from a magazine, but it was a start.

The sound of running water caught his attention. He was used to listening for Miranda but this time he knew it was Rory. In the shower? The thought tumbled though his mind before he could squash it.

The water stopped. Not the shower. *Not that it's any of your business,* he told himself, wishing he hadn't already formed a clear mental picture of Rory's long wet blond hair falling over her bare shoulders.

"Get a life," he said out loud to himself, even though he had no intention of following his own advice. The existence he had right now *was* his life.

Parenting, he reminded himself. That was what he should be thinking about. The article on teaching children to be tactful might be helpful. Was it possible to teach a child not to blurt out things like, *Then she died and we stopped going for ice cream?* Considering that certain adults didn't mind talking about where they'd been conceived, wanting a child to be tactful seemed like a high expectation. Again, he tried to focus on the magazine. A health topic, like the item titled "Bye-bye Baby Teeth" might be easier to master. Especially since it seemed that for the next few years, he'd have to keep the tooth fairy on retainer.

The floorboards creaked directly overhead, followed by the sound of metal on metal and finally a dull thunk. Rory was opening the Murphy bed. Until that instant it hadn't occurred to him that she'd be sleeping directly above him. She'd said she didn't have a boyfriend, but what if she got one? What if he started spending the night here? There. Up there, in her bed. No way could he lie here listening to moaning bedsprings and whatever other sounds went with Rory being made love to.

Mitch groaned, not wanting to think about her sprawling naked on the bed, especially not with some other guy. He could certainly picture himself with her. Even before the idea was fully formed, he rolled the magazine into a tube and batted himself on the head with it.

Maybe he really did need to get a life, or at least get out a bit more. In spite of Miranda's assumption that someday he'd marry again, he wasn't ready for the dating scene. But a couple of guys from the station had been after him to go for a beer after their basketball game. When Laura was alive, he'd always wanted to get home after the game. After the accident, he hadn't liked leaving Miranda with a sitter any longer than necessary, but now that they were living here, what could it hurt? Tomorrow morning he'd check to see if his mother would be available to sit with Miranda. It was time he stopped making excuses and started living again.

Chapter Six

Mitch kept a firm grip on his daughter's slender little hand as they waited for a walk signal to cross Powell Street. She was old enough to know better than to rush into traffic, but he felt better knowing she was there at his side, safe and secure.

"Have you ever been to an art opening, Dad?"

"No, I haven't."

"Me either. Miss Sunshine said there'd be wine an' cheese."

"You're a little young to be drinking wine," Mitch teased.

Miranda giggled. "I wonder if there'll be pop. I can have some if there is, right?"

"Sure. It's a special occasion. But just a small glass, okay? Or maybe there'll be juice." Laura hadn't wanted their daughter eating a lot of junk food.

"You already said yes to pop. You can't change your mind."

"I won't. But just one," he said, doing his best to sound firm.

"I hope there'll be other stuff to eat besides cheese. I only like orange cheese, not the stinky white stuff that Grams buys."

He had to agree with that. "They might have orange cheese."

"I hope they have cookies."

Wine and cookies? He doubted it, but what the heck. Aside from the breakfast cereal he bought, his mother kept the house stocked with health food, most of it organic. Miranda had a healthy diet. How much harm could there be in a glass of pop and a couple of cookies?

His mother's boyfriend, Thomas, had picked up Rory and his mother and they'd gone downtown to have dinner with Annie McGaskell and Copper Pennington. He and Miranda had been invited to join them, but he had declined. He wasn't ready to spend that much time with their new neighbor. He felt a little bit out of control when he was around her, and that scared the hell out of him. Luckily, Miranda hadn't been around when the dinner invitation was extended. She would have begged to go along, and he had a hard time saying no to her.

Rory had been living upstairs for less than two weeks, but it felt like much longer. In a good way, mostly. Miranda talked nonstop about her, declaring she was the best teacher ever, his mother claimed she was the best tenant she'd ever had, and he was slowly coming around to agreeing on both counts. Miranda seemed to be behaving at school, which meant no unexpected phone calls from the teacher, and he was grateful for that. He'd also developed the habit of checking to see if her van was parked on the street, and wondering when she'd be home if it wasn't. In a nonstalkerish way, he hoped.

For the past year, he'd often tried to figure out how Laura would have handled their daughter in a given situation. Now he also found himself wondering what Rory would do. Although she had insisted she didn't want a family of her own, she had a natural, comfortable way with children that he envied.

A cable car jangled past and, as if on cue, Miranda

brightened. "Will you ever want to go for a cable-car ride?" she asked.

"We'll do it one of these days."

"When?"

He sighed. At least the familiar old sound hadn't made him feel as though he was suffocating. "I'm not sure." And that was the truth.

He had assumed the exhibit would be at the Museum of Modern Art, but it was at a private gallery near Union Square. The place was all windows, and from the sidewalk across the street he could see it was already teeming with art aficionados. He hated crowds.

"Look," Miranda said, pointing at the gallery across the street. "I can see Miss Sunshine. And Grams and Thomas and Annie."

Mitch squeezed his daughter's hand. He had already spotted Rory. She stood near a window with the others, but she might as well have been alone. As she laughed and glanced animatedly from one companion to another, her long hair swung around her shoulders and reflected the light. Was she aware that she stood out from the rest of the crowd? In a good way, of course. He was pretty sure she wasn't. She was definitely the only person he knew who could wear turquoise pants with a lime-green jacket, and make it work. From where he stood, he couldn't tell what she had on her feet, but he had a hunch he was going to like it.

His mother had her arm linked with Thomas's. It had taken Mitch a while to get used to his mother having another man in her life, but he was slowly coming around to the idea. Thomas was a quiet, thoughtful man who'd spent his working life as a reporter for the *San Francisco Chronicle,* and who wrote poetry in his spare time. Mitch had read some of it, and he'd taken his mother's word that it was good. Thomas had a full head of unruly gray hair and a beard to match, which reminded Miranda of Santa Claus. Next to Thomas and Betsy, Annie's petite stature made her look like an elf.

When the light turned green Mitch and his daughter crossed the street and went inside. San Francisco was full of art lovers, and judging by the size of this crowd, Copper Pennington's work was well-known. The throng was shoulder-to-shoulder, and the place was abuzz with conversation and anticipation. Mitch took a quick inventory of the fire exits.

"Do you like Rory's mom's paintings, Dad?"

"They're very...colorful." They were modern or abstract or whatever the term was, and huge. Floor-to-ceiling huge.

"Can you see stuff in them?"

He had no idea what she was talking about. "What kind of stuff?"

"Like in the clouds. Miss Sunshine says if you look at her mother's paintings long enough, you'll see animal shapes and other things like that."

He searched the closest painting, wishing this sort of thing didn't make him feel as uncomfortable as it did. He had no imagination and he didn't mind admitting it, but it was also possible that he couldn't see anything in this painting because it wasn't there.

After they joined his mother and Thomas, Annie and Rory, the conversation focused around Miranda's excited chatter, giving him a moment to surreptitiously check out Rory's footwear. Lime-green sandals, turquoise toe polish and a gold toe ring. He was pretty sure his heart missed a couple of beats.

When he looked up, she was smiling at him. "I'm so

glad you two could make it. My mother is looking forward to meeting you."

He was intrigued by the prospect of meeting her, too. He took a quick look around to see if he could spot her. He imagined she'd be tall and blond, like her daughter, and probably wearing something even more outrageous, in keeping with her paintings. Maybe a long, flowing caftan or something. If people still wore caftans.

Finally, Rory raised an arm and waved exuberantly. "Mom! Over here!"

Mitch couldn't identify the object of her enthusiastic gesture until the crowd parted and a tiny, small-boned woman emerged. She was wearing a pair of extremely wide-legged black pants, a high-necked, hip-length tunic affair made of patchwork—a quilt?—and shoes with ridiculously high heels. Even with the several extra inches, she barely cleared Rory's shoulder when the two of them embraced.

With voluminous hair in an orange-red shade that surely didn't occur in nature, she more than lived up to her name. Mitch doubted she'd had the name or the hair since birth, but she was as beautiful as her daughter and she looked exactly like the kind of woman who would name her child Sunshine.

"So?" she said to Rory. "What do you think?"

"Definitely your best work ever. I love every single one of them."

"Have you picked your favorite?"

Rory laughed. "Trust me, Mom. *None* of these will fit in my apartment, but I especially love the canvas behind the reception desk. The one that looks like a pod of whales surfacing at sunset."

"That's one of my favorites, too. It's called *California Gray*. I'll have them mark it sold and we'll keep it at my place until you have room for it."

Mitch stared hard at the painting. Gray whales? He assumed that was what she meant. And a sunset? All he saw were huge splashes of dark blue and red and orange paint.

"I have a canvas from each of my mother's series," Rory told them.

That explained all the artwork he'd carried upstairs when she moved in.

She placed a hand on Miranda's shoulder. "Mom, this is Betsy's son, Mitch, and his daughter, Miranda."

Copper extended her multi-ringed hand. "Ah, yes. The firefighter." Then she shifted her attention to Miranda and smiled. "And what do you do?"

She giggled. "I go to school. I'm in Miss Sunshine's class."

"You are? Is she a good teacher?"

"The awesomest!"

"I thought she would be. Do you like art?" Copper asked.

Miranda's head bobbed excitedly. "We do art at school, and Miss Sunshine's bringing us here on a field trip next week."

"So I hear."

"Did you paint all these pictures yourself?" Miranda asked.

"Yes, I did. What do you think of them?"

"I think they're very watery, like the ocean."

Copper's smile indicated she was impressed. "That's an excellent observation. I was thinking about the ocean when I painted them."

She shifted her attention to Mitch. "She's very perceptive for someone so young."

He was tempted to tell her that Miranda didn't get it from him, but he had a hunch Copper Pennington already had him pegged. Before he could think of something intelligent-sounding to say about her paintings, they were joined by a tall, intellectual-looking man and a young, hip-looking woman.

"Dad? What are you doing here?"

Rory hadn't said anything about her father joining them, and her surprise suggested she hadn't been expecting him. In an instant, Copper's demeanor switched from warm to icy. Her greeting was a single word.

"Sam."

If his appearance caught her off guard, she wasn't letting on.

Rory hugged her father warmly, but when she spoke to her mother, there was a hint of accusation in her tone.

"Did you know he was coming?"

"Of course. He knows better than to show up at one of my openings unannounced."

"Why didn't you tell me?"

"He asked me not to."

"I wanted to surprise you," Sam said. "And I wish the two of you wouldn't talk about me as though I'm not in the room."

Copper gave him a wry smile. "If you'd rather we talked behind your back—"

"Okay, okay, okay," Rory said. "Let's be nice."

"*Nice* isn't in your mother's vocabulary."

Copper ignored the jibe and studied his much-younger companion instead. "At least I'm not—"

Rory cut off her mother's response. "For heaven's sake, stop. Please."

She made another round of introductions and while she did, Mitch took stock of the newcomers. Rory's father was as carefully put together as his ex-wife, albeit very differently. If he was deliberately striving to look literary, he'd succeeded. Longish salt-and-pepper hair pulled back into a ponytail. Bifocals low on his nose. Black turtleneck. Charcoal tweed jacket with suede elbow patches. Blue jeans. His only accessory was the stunning young brunette on his arm.

"I'd like everyone to meet my assistant, Daisy Dumont," he said.

"It's spelled *D-a-y-z-e-e.*" She smiled as though she was revealing a secret.

D-a-y-z-e-e? What was wrong with *D-a-i-s-y?* At least with that she wouldn't have to go through life spelling her name every time she was introduced.

Sam made a pretense of taking Dayzee's hand in his. "Copper. You're looking well."

Between Rory, her mother and the girlfriend, Mitch wondered who would strangle Sam first. He usually was not a fan of family drama, but this was more interesting than art. Especially *this* art, because no matter how long or how hard he stared at these paintings, he couldn't make out anything familiar. At some point he would have to say something to the artist, and he had no idea what that would be.

These are mighty big paintings for such a small woman. Even he knew better than that.

Nice use of color. Duh.

Go ahead and strangle him. Yep. Under the circumstances, that seemed most fitting.

"Did you fire your last assistant or did she find a real job?" Copper asked.

Ouch.

Sam didn't respond.

Her next comment was addressed to Dayzee. "How's the book-writing business these days?"

The young woman looked completely at a loss, making it

clear that whatever she did to "assist" Sam, it didn't involve his literary pursuits.

Sam seemed to take his wife's barbs in stride. "Dayzee's on my PR team."

"How nice. What's your specialty, Dayzee?" Copper asked. "Reader satisfaction?"

Rory elbowed her mother, and Mitch found himself feeling sorry for her. If this was an indication of what her family life had been like, no wonder she'd sworn off having one of her own.

Dayzee gave them all a benign smile. She didn't look offended, probably because she missed the innuendo. "Your daughter is adorable," she said to Rory, giving Sam's arm a playful swat. "Naughty man. You didn't tell me you were a grandfather."

It was a few seconds before it dawned on Mitch that she thought Rory was Miranda's mother, and then he had a hard time drawing a breath.

Rory broke the stunned silence. "I don't have children. This is Mitch's daughter."

Dayzee mustn't have been paying attention when they were introduced.

Miranda, who had started to fidget, tugged on her grandmother's sleeve and whispered something to her.

"Excuse us," Betsy said. "We need to find a washroom."

Mitch nodded his thanks to his mother as she hustled Miranda away. Thomas and Annie took advantage of the opportunity to escape with them. After they left, a tall middle-aged woman with a gallery name tag pinned to the lapel of her gray blazer approached them. "Ms. Pennington? We'd like to get started in about ten minutes. Is there anything you need?"

"I should check the podium."

"Good idea. I'll help you get set up."

"Rory, would you come with me? I'm giving a brief introduction to the show and I'd like you to check my notes."

If it was an excuse to get Rory away from her father, it worked. The three women walked away, leaving Mitch with Sam and Dayzee.

"I totally see what you mean about how impossible she is," Dayzee said.

Given that Copper's former husband had shown up with a woman young enough to be his daughter, Mitch had admired her restraint.

"Welcome to my world," Sam said, but he wasn't looking at Dayzee. He craned his neck a little, his gaze still on Copper, even though she was now by the podium on the other side of the gallery and partly obscured by the crowd. Dayzee kept talking, but Sam seemed only to have eyes for his wife. Ex-wife.

Dayzee tapped Sam's shoulder. "I'm going to look for the little girls' room. Would you be a sweetie and get me a drink?"

Sam dragged his attention back to her. "What would you like?"

"I'd like a vodka Collins, but I'll bet all they have is wine."

"Red or white?"

She shrugged. "White, I guess." She swung away and disappeared into the crowd.

"Sorry about that," Sam said after she was out of earshot. "Copper and I like to push each other's buttons."

No kidding. Mitch mustered a smile that probably didn't come close to looking sincere.

"She's a spitfire." Sam's gaze briefly followed Dayzee, then returned to Rory's mother.

Mitch wondered which woman he was referring to. Maybe both. But Rory's family dynamics were none of his business, so he wracked his brain for something else to say. "My wife loved your books."

Sam gave him a thoughtful look. "You said that in the past tense."

Damn it. Should have played it safe and talked about the weather. "Oh. She, ah, passed away. Car accident."

"Sorry to hear that."

Mitch nodded.

Sam glanced awkwardly around the gallery. "I'd better get Dayzee's drink. Can I get you something? A glass of wine?"

"No, thanks. I'm driving."

"Right."

"You go ahead. I'll wait for my daughter."

Sam headed for the bar, and Mitch relaxed a little. He shouldn't have mentioned Laura. The idea of a young mother losing her life always made people uncomfortable.

The next half hour was mercifully uneventful. Miranda returned with two crackers, some orange cheese and a handful of carrot sticks on a napkin, while his mother carried the much-anticipated glass of pop. To Mitch's relief, Sam and Dayzee didn't rejoin them. He could see them across the gallery, talking to Rory.

After Copper was introduced, Mitch picked up his daughter so she could see the podium. True to her word, Copper's remarks were brief but enlightening. The paintings had been inspired by her home on the northern California coast. The size of the canvases represented the majesty of the marine mammals, especially the gray whales' annual migration.

He glanced at his watch and realized it was well past Miranda's usual bedtime. He checked with his mother to be

sure Thomas was driving her home, half expecting Miranda
to plead for more time, but she only had one request.

"We have to say goodbye to Miss Sunshine."

No argument there. He scanned the room and spotted her
standing in front of the painting that was now part of her
private collection. He and Miranda squeezed past several
groups of people to get to her.

"Miss Sunshine! G'bye! We're going home."

Rory checked her watch. "Oh, my. It *is* getting late.
Would you mind giving me a ride? My mom's hosting a
private cocktail party when this is over, but that'll be too
late for me."

"No problem." No problem at all.

"Yippee!" Miranda said, bouncing up and down.

"I'll see my mom tomorrow, but I need to say goodbye
to my father. He leaves for L.A. first thing in the morning.
Just give me one minute."

Mitch hung back while she said her goodbyes, but he
was acutely aware of Sam's scrutiny when Rory said she
was going home with him. He knew what she meant by
"home," but did Sam?

Powell Street was still bustling when they stepped outside, but it seemed quieter and less claustrophobic than the
gallery. They walked the three blocks to where he'd parked,
while he listened to Miranda's chatter and occasionally
responded to it. He hoped she wouldn't mention the cable
car as it rolled down the street to the turntable, and for once
her attention had been diverted.

He held her hand, and he saw her stick the other into
Miss Sunshine's while she babbled about something that
happened at school that day. For a couple of very intense
moments, he felt connected, part of a family again, and
he knew they looked like one. They were even walking in
unison. Dayzee had assumed Rory was Miranda's mother,

likely because their hair color was so similar. By default, that meant Dayzee had also assumed Rory was his wife. Nothing could be further from the truth, but that didn't stop him from pondering the possibilities that might present themselves after Miranda was asleep. He glanced down at Rory's turquoise-polished toes and knew exactly where those possibilities would start.

Chapter Seven

Late Friday afternoon, Rory trudged up the two flights of stairs to her apartment with her overstuffed school bag, two sacks of groceries and some great finds from a vintage clothing store she'd discovered. She'd splurged on a trio of red, white and black Bakelite bangles, and she had also found an outrageous pair of pink marabou mules for playing dress-up with Miranda. She was seriously out of breath when she finally reached the top of the stairs and unlocked the door to her apartment.

Buick was sprawled on his back on the sofa.

"You lazy old cat," she said.

He blinked twice, yawned and closed his eyes again.

Rory dumped her bags on the kitchen table and gave Buick a belly rub on her way to the other end of the apartment, shedding her school clothes as she went. She flung her plum-colored slacks and gold shirt over the back of a chair, kicked her shoes into the closet, and pulled on a comfy pair of black exercise pants and a white camisole. The air in the apartment felt a little chilly, though, so she pulled a bright red boat-necked sweater over top. She enjoyed being cozy and casual at home as much as she loved putting together dressy outfits for school.

She put away the groceries and tossed the DVD she'd rented onto the coffee table. Then she took the jewelry and shoes out of the thrift-store bag and slipped the bracelets onto her wrist. The colors were perfect with what she was wearing so she left them on. The shoes were over-the-top crazy, but she slipped them on, too. They definitely did not go with her outfit, but they were still fun and she was sure Miranda would be delighted with them.

Would the little girl's father approve? Rory looked down at her feet. Thinking about what Mitch might think of these shoes made her smile. She left them on and opened a fresh can of cat food. Buick immediately rolled off the sofa, meowing as though he hadn't eaten in a month and rubbing himself against her calves while she scooped the food into his bowl.

"Are you hungry?" she asked. "Me, too." While he ate, she heated a can of vegetable soup and made a grilled cheese sandwich. When they were ready, she pushed aside some magazines and junk mail on the coffee table, set down her soup mug and plate, and settled onto the sofa.

"Friday night and I get to do whatever I want." It would be nice to have a date once in a while, though. Maybe she'd meet someone at Nic and Jonathan's wedding. While she sipped her soup, she read the back of the DVD case. Since she didn't have plans tonight, she'd settle for staying home with Colin Firth.

"A girl can dream," she said to Buick. He ignored her. He had finished eating and was busy licking a paw and swiping it over one ear. He paused momentarily at a sound from the stairwell.

Rory sat up straighter and listened. Were those footsteps?

Yes.

They were too heavy to be Miranda's. Could it be Mitch?

She smoothed her hair and shrugged off the wide neck

of the sweater to expose one shoulder. She didn't intend to flirt with him, but she was a woman and it felt good to be around a man who was attracted to her. Especially when the feeling was mutual.

Tap, tap, tap.

She tucked the feathery pink shoes under the coffee table, thinking this might not be the time to test his reaction to them, and went to open the door.

It wasn't Mitch. It was his mother.

Rory hitched her sweater back onto her shoulder and silently scolded herself for acting like a schoolgirl.

"I'm sorry to bother you," Betsy said. "Thomas was given two theatre tickets and invited me to see a play with him. It's very last-minute and I'd love to go, but Mitch is out tonight and it's too late to find a sitter. I was wondering—" She paused, as though reluctant to ask.

"If I'll sit with her?" Rory volunteered. "I'll be happy to."

"You're sure? You don't have plans?"

"It's been a hectic week and I have a busy day tomorrow, so I decided to stay in and watch a movie. If you have a DVD player, I can just as easily watch it at your place."

"Mitch brought one when he and Miranda moved in, but I don't know how to use it."

"I can figure it out. Should I come down right now?"

"No, I don't have to leave for half an hour. Take your time," Betsy said. "I really appreciate this, and I won't make a habit of asking. In fact, if Mitch gets home before I do…" Her voice trailed off.

"Don't worry. I'll tell him it was my idea." Rory doubted very much that Mitch ever asked for help, but that didn't mean his mother shouldn't.

"Thanks. This play has had great reviews, and I hate to turn down free tickets."

"It's not a problem. I'm happy to help out if I can."

"Thanks. I really appreciate this." Before Betsy left, she took a quick look around the apartment. "How's everything up here? Do you have enough storage space?"

Rory glanced back and surveyed the clutter with fresh eyes. The place was a disaster. "Everything's perfect. I've been working on fall decorations for my classroom and I'm helping with a bridal shower for my friend who's getting married."

"That explains it," Betsy said. "I'll let you get back to what you were doing. See you in half an hour."

Rory finished eating and added her plate and mug to the other dishes in the kitchen sink. She grabbed a package of microwave popcorn from the cupboard, picked up the DVD and slipped her feet into a pair of red flip-flops that matched the polish she'd applied the other day.

Buick jumped onto the sofa and curled up in the spot she'd just vacated. "Don't wait up," she said as she grabbed her things off the table and dashed down the stairs.

BETSY HAD LEFT HER DOOR from the front foyer open. "Hello?" Rory called.

"Miss Sunshine's here!" Miranda, dressed in a yellow nightgown that ended several inches above her ankles, emerged from a hallway and bounded across the living room. "Can I stay up an extra half hour, Grams? Please? Please, please, please?"

Betsy was right behind her. "Maybe next time if we check with your dad, but not tonight. My son is not very flexible about bedtime," she added for Rory's benefit.

"Routines are great," Rory said. "What time is bedtime?"

"Eight o'clock."

Rory glanced at her watch. "That's a whole half hour,"

she said, ruffling Miranda's blond curls. "What would you like to do?"

"Stay up till nine o'clock."

"Eight," Betsy repeated. "Now give Grams a hug and a good-night kiss, then I'll leave you two girls to have some fun."

"G'night, Grams. Love you."

"Love you, too, Miranda."

The affectionate exchange between grandmother and granddaughter impressed Rory. This little girl might not have a mother, but she had lots of love and stability.

Betsy glanced out the living-room window. "Here's Thomas. See you later."

"What would you like to do?" she asked Miranda after Betsy left. "We have time for a game or we can read a book."

"A book," Miranda said without hesitation. She grabbed Rory's hand and tugged her through the living room, down the hallway and through the kitchen. Near the back door, a set of stairs led to the second floor. Miranda sprinted up the stairs ahead of her. Rory followed, taking her time to look around once they were upstairs. There appeared to be three bedrooms and a bathroom. The first room on the right, with old oak furniture and an appealing patchwork quilt, must be Betsy's. The room across the hall was Miranda's and the bathroom was next to it. The room at the front of the house must be Mitch's. Did she dare sneak a peek?

No. She followed Miranda into her bedroom. "Wow. What a beautiful room."

"I picked out the wallpaper," the little girl said.

"It's very pretty." The paper had a charming, old-fashioned look—a pale-yellow background covered with tiny dark yellow flowers and bright green leaves. The woodwork had been painted a gleaming white to match the furniture, and a green area rug covered most of the hardwood floor. Very grown-up for a seven-year-old. Rory wondered if she'd had a little guidance.

"Me and Grams went to the paint store together, but she let me choose. I picked this 'cause yellow is my mom's favorite color."

Aha. That explained a lot, and it was interesting that Miranda referred to her mother's preferences in the present tense.

"My dad put up the wallpaper and Grams painted."

"I see," Rory said. Moving to a new home and a new school could be unsettling for a child, so Mitch and his mother had been wise to let her have some say in her bedroom decor. "I think you picked the perfect wallpaper. I'll bet your mom would love this room."

"D'you think so? I asked my dad if he thought she would, but he doesn't like to talk about her."

"He must miss her," Rory said.

"So do I, but talking about her doesn't make me sad."

"Lucky thing he's got you. I can tell he's very proud of you." The conversation was quickly turning personal, and she already knew Mitch well enough to know he wouldn't be happy that his daughter and his daughter's teacher were having this conversation. "Now where's that book you want to read?"

Miranda crouched in front of a crammed bookcase. "I have a *lot* of books."

"I see that. Do you have a favorite?"

"Could you read Harry Potter? My mom was going to read it to me, but she died before we got started." She pulled the book from the shelf and handed it to Rory.

This felt like dangerous territory. Reading the book might seem as though she was trying to be a substitute for

Miranda's mother, which couldn't be further from the truth. "Maybe your dad would rather read it with you."

Miranda firmly shook her head. "He says Harry Potter was Mom's book. He likes to read Winnie the Pooh, though. He always makes me laugh 'cause he does different voices for all the animals."

Rory tried to imagine that.

Hi, my name is Tigger. T-i-double-guh-er.

No.

Eeyore, no problem. Tigger? Not so much.

"I think we should ask your dad about Harry Potter." She slid the book back into place and took out an illustrated copy of *Cinderella*. "This is one of my favorites. I love fairy tales."

"Me, too." Miranda ran a hand over Cinderella's ball gown on the cover. "This is like your pink bridesmaid dress, only yours is prettier."

"Wait'll you see the new one," she said. "It has a big wide skirt."

"What color is it?"

"Blue."

"Like the sky?"

No. The blue of those dresses was startlingly unnatural. "A little brighter than that."

"Can we still play dress-up sometime?"

"You bet. Someday when your dad and your grandmother are busy, you can spend the day with me. We can pretend we're princesses having tea with the queen." She considered telling her about the shoes, but decided to let them be a surprise.

"Can we have *real* tea?" Miranda asked.

"For sure." Although she'd need to make sure that was okay with Mitch. "We can even shop for cookies and petit fours to have with it."

Miranda looked confused. "What are petty fours?"

"Petit fours are tiny little cakes covered with frosting and decorations. They look just like regular cakes, except you get to have one all to yourself. *Petit* is the French word for 'small.'"

Miranda's eyes went wide. "Can we have ice cream with them?" Since last Saturday, she had mentioned ice cream and the trip to Fisherman's Wharf several times.

"You like ice cream a lot, don't you?"

Miranda's head bobbed up and down. "Really a lot."

"Then we'll have some with our tea and cookies."

"And petit fours."

"Right. Now, how about that bedtime story?"

"'Kay."

"Have you brushed your teeth?"

"Yup." Miranda tugged at the comforter on her bed. "All except the loose one. It's too wiggly to brush." She demonstrated its looseness by moving it back and forth with the tip of her tongue.

Rory laughed and held up the comforter so Miranda could crawl under the covers.

Miranda tried to pile her pillows against the headboard. "If we put the pillows like this, you can sit beside me so I can see the pictures."

"Here, let me help."

"Perfect," Miranda said, once the pillows had been stacked to her liking.

Rory tucked the sheet and comforter around the little girl, then sat on the bed and leaned against the pillows. "Comfy?"

"Mm-hm."

"Once upon a time…" Rory started as she opened the book, but she wasn't thinking about fairy tales. She was completely blown away by the feel of a little girl's head resting on her shoulder and the honeysuckle-scented curls brushing her cheek.

TWENTY MINUTES LATER the story was over and Miranda was struggling to keep her eyes open. Rory stood up and slipped the book back onto the shelf.

"Good night, Miranda."

Two small arms flew out from under the covers. "Hug?"

"Of course." Rory leaned over and accepted the hug, then dropped a kiss on the soft, smooth skin of the little girl's forehead. "Sweet dreams."

"Daddy always says 'sleep tight.'"

"My father used to say that to me, too." She straightened and backed away.

"Dads *always* say stuff like that."

Rory wondered if Miranda's mother had a favorite bedtime saying. "Should I turn off the hall light?" she asked instead.

"No, thanks. My dad waits till I go to sleep, then he turns it off."

Rory could imagine him coming into the room to check on his little girl and then turning out the hall light. For such a big, reserved man, he had a surprisingly gentle side, at least when it came to Miranda. Losing his wife had probably left him vulnerable, too, and he'd overcompensated by shutting down his emotions. He was a good father, though, no question about that, and Rory couldn't help wondering what kind of husband he'd been. Very traditional, from what Betsy had told her.

From the doorway, she glanced back at Mitch's daughter. "Good night," she said again.

This time there was no reply. Miranda was already asleep.

Rory left the bedroom door open so she could hear the little girl if she woke up. She glanced down the hallway in the direction of Mitch's bedroom. Should she give in to curiosity? No way. It was one thing to be curious. Snooping was just plain dumb.

Downstairs, she took the DVD and the popcorn out of the bag she'd left in the living room. She tossed the DVD onto the coffee table and peeled the plastic wrapper off the popcorn package on her way to the kitchen. After she stuck it in the microwave, she spotted a nested set of blue-glazed pottery bowls on a shelf above the counter. She reached for them, discovered they were a lot heavier than they looked, and had to do some quick maneuvering to avoid dropping them.

The popping stopped and she dumped the steaming contents of the bag into the medium-size bowl and inhaled. "Smells good," she said as she headed to the living room. "Sorry to keep you waiting, Colin."

It was late when Mitch drove down the block and hit the garage-door opener clipped to the visor. Rory's van was parked in front of the house, but that didn't mean she was here, he reminded himself. He glanced up at her dark window. More than likely she was out with her friends and would be taking a cab home.

How is that any of your business? Whenever he was at home, he found himself speculating about where Rory was or what she was doing. If anyone else had been doing that, he'd say it sounded like an obsession. Lucky for him no one else knew about it, and he knew it wasn't.

He pulled into the garage and stepped out of his car as the door rolled shut behind him. He took off his jacket as he climbed the stairs to the kitchen, surprised to find all the lights on. His mother was militant about keeping lights turned off when no one was in the room. He flicked off the switch and went down the hallway to the living room. The lights in there were on, too, and he could hear the television.

It wasn't like her to be watching TV on a Friday night. Or ever, for that matter.

But not even the blazing lights and blaring TV prepared him for the sight of the woman asleep on the sofa. Rory's head rested on a small cushion and her long blond hair streamed over her shoulders, veiling what might otherwise be a breathtaking bit of cleavage. A patchwork quilt covered everything from the waist down. Everything but the red-polished toes of one foot.

He closed his eyes and struggled to take a breath. The night before Laura had died, he had played basketball with the guys and come home to find her sleeping on the sofa. He'd carried her upstairs and they'd made love. It had been the last time he'd had intimate contact with another human being, and it felt like an eternity ago. Standing in his mother's living room, watching Rory sleep, he didn't think he'd ever missed his wife more.

What was Rory doing here? He moved into the room, which must have startled her because she suddenly sat bolt upright.

"Oh!" She stared up at him with panic-filled eyes. "I must've fallen asleep." As she brushed her hair back from her face, several plastic bracelets clattered on her wrist. Her red sweater had slipped off one shoulder, exposing a thin white shoulder strap and the upper curve of one spectacular breast.

"Sorry," he said, using his jacket to hide his reaction to her bare skin. "I didn't mean to startle you. I was expecting to see my mother." Then it dawned on him that maybe he should be concerned. "Where is she? Is everything okay?"

"Everything's fine. Thomas scored some free theater tickets and I didn't have plans so I said I'd stay with Miranda."

He'd been afraid this sort of thing might happen. "You know, just because you're living upstairs doesn't mean you should feel obligated—"

"Don't worry about it. It would have been a shame for her to miss the play and since I wasn't going out, I was happy to help. All I'd planned to do tonight was watch a movie, so I brought it with me." She swung her legs off the sofa and sat up.

He tossed his jacket over the back of a chair, relieved to have regained most of his self-control. "Would you like some coffee?" he asked. He hoped she'd say yes. After this unexpected encounter, it'd be a while before he'd be able to sleep.

"As long as it's decaf. Otherwise I'll never get back to sleep tonight."

"Decaf it is." Although he knew what might cure her insomnia. And his. "I'll be right back."

She grabbed the bowl from the coffee table and followed him into the kitchen. "I made myself some popcorn. I'd better wash this and put it away."

She waited while he filled the coffeepot, and he was intensely aware of her standing behind him. After he moved away from the sink, she dumped a few stray kernels into the trash, washed the bowl, and dried it while he scooped coffee into the filter basket and turned on the machine.

Rory stood on her toes and tried to heft the bowls back onto the shelf. They were heavy—he had no idea why his mother kept them up there.

"Let me help." His hand collided with hers and they both jerked away, tipping the bowls off the shelf.

He grabbed for them. She grabbed them. Their arms ended up tangled together and somehow the pottery was caught within them.

"Don't let go," she said. "I don't have a very good grip."

He didn't seem to have a grip on anything, least of all the damn bowls.

She laughed up at him as she freed one hand and placed it under the largest. "There. That's better."

She was already too close for comfort and her sweet, citrus scent tugged at him like a magnet. Her shoulder was exposed again, and he'd never really paid attention to her eyes before, except to note that they were blue, but now he noticed the tiny flecks of black and silver.

Her smile faded and her gaze became more cautious. "You can let go now."

"You sure?"

"I'm sure."

He carefully extracted one hand and then the other, being careful not to upset her balance.

She set the bowls on the counter and pulled her sweater back up over her shoulder before she restacked them.

"Let me put them back for you."

"Okay." But she didn't move away, and he had the impression it was deliberate.

He safely returned the bowls to their home on the shelf, and then he stood his ground. Not that he had any intention of making a move, but he was suddenly curious to find out if she would.

"The coffee smells great," she said.

He glanced at the coffeemaker and back at her. "Still a couple of minutes till it's ready."

He couldn't remember the last time he'd been alone with a woman. To make matters worse, he was terrible at making small talk. What were they going to do while they waited?

"I don't think it would be a good idea," she said.

"What?"

"For you to kiss me."

"Excuse me?"

"You were thinking about kissing me, and I'm telling you it's not a good idea."

"No, I wasn't."

She was looking at him as though she knew otherwise.

That was *not* what he'd been thinking. Was it? He was pretty sure he hadn't had a coherent thought since he'd walked in and found her asleep on the sofa, but damn it, now that she'd suggested it, kissing her was all he could think about.

"I'm Miranda's teacher, your mother's tenant and we live in the same house. It would be way too complicated."

Finally, something they agreed on. "You've got that right." He moved away and grabbed a couple of coffee mugs out of a cupboard.

"I should go," she said.

He didn't want that either. "The coffee's ready, and it'll be nice to have someone to talk to. I promise I won't…" He couldn't bring himself to say it out loud, but they both knew what he meant. He hoped she'd stay.

"Okay."

The coffeemaker sputtered out the last few drops. He filled the two mugs and handed one to her. "Milk?"

"Black is fine, thanks."

"After you," he said, gesturing toward the living room.

She curled up on one end of the sofa and pulled the old quilt over her legs. Too bad. He liked looking at those feet. He set his coffee on a small table, settled himself in the oversize armchair and lifted his feet onto the ottoman.

"Did you have a date tonight?" she asked.

He suspected she was baiting him, but he couldn't tell for sure. "No. I was playing basketball with friends."

"I see. Did you win?"

"We did. One of the guys on the team said he knows you."

"Oh." For a split second, a look that was awfully close to guilt flashed across her face. "I'll bet that was my friend's fiancé, Jonathan. They're getting married in a couple of weeks. I'm her bridesmaid. Maid of honor, actually."

"That's what he said."

"Did he say anything else?"

Plenty. He'd said Rory was an interesting woman. No, *remarkable* had been the word he'd used. And damned attractive, didn't Mitch think? Yes, he'd agreed she was. There'd also been several hints about Rory being single, unattached and available.

He drank some of his coffee and shook his head in answer to her question. "No. Just that you were in the wedding party."

Rory looked relieved. "That's good."

Interesting. Even to Mitch, who wasn't too swift about figuring these things out, it was obvious that Rory and Jonathan's fiancée had been talking about him. Did he dare consider what that conversation had been about? Definitely not. Besides, as she'd just said, this could get complicated.

"Did you have any trouble getting Miranda to go to sleep?" he asked instead.

"Not at all. She wanted to stay up past her bedtime but Betsy didn't think you'd agree so she said no. We read *Cinderella* and she was practically asleep by the end of the story, so I doubt if she could have stayed awake, even if she'd tried."

"My mother thinks I have too many rules." At the same time, it was reassuring to know she was willing to go along with them, even when he wasn't here to enforce them.

Rory's sweater slid off her shoulder and she shrugged it

back into place again. "I wouldn't call that being strict at all. I'm not a parent, but I do know something about kids. Like I said to your mom, they thrive on routines. I think you're doing the right thing."

Part of him wished she'd leave the shoulder exposed. Her skin looked warm and inviting, and he was intrigued by the possibility of what that white strap might be attached to. "That's not what you said when you called about Miranda fighting with that other kid at school."

Rory looked confused. "What did I say?"

To be honest, he couldn't remember. "I'm not sure. I just got the impression you thought I was a lousy parent."

"Mitch, I'm sorry. Nothing could be further from the truth. This can't be easy, but she's a great kid. Whatever you're doing, it's working. Oh, I left the hall light on because I figured you'd want to check on her when you got home."

"Thanks for keeping an eye on her." He wondered if he should offer to pay her for babysitting.

"No problem. I enjoy spending time with her." Her bracelets clattered as she lifted her mug to her lips.

He tried to cover a yawn, hoping she wouldn't notice.

She did. "I should go." She pushed the quilt aside and stood up. There went the sweater again.

Instinctively he got up, too, narrowly avoiding a collision as she rounded the coffee table and started across the room.

She quickly stepped to one side. "I'll just get my movie out of your DVD player."

"Oh, sure." He took a step sideways, too, and this time they connected. "Sorry," he said, wishing he'd stayed seated instead of trying to be a gentleman. And then he wished he could kiss her, no matter how complicated that might be.

The way Rory was looking at him, he half expected

another mini-lecture on why kissing was a bad idea. She didn't say anything, though, and he was caught in her gaze like a deer in the headlights of a semi. And then his hands, which seemed to develop a mind of their own, were on her shoulders and her arms were around his neck.

"This is still not a good idea," he said.

She touched her cheek to his. "I know, but everyone can use a hug now and then."

His needs were so far past hugging, it wasn't even funny. Her crazy sweater slid sideways again and all that bare skin was within nuzzling distance. She tossed her head and her hair brushed the back of his hand. She pulled a little bit away so that their bodies weren't touching, except for her hands on his shoulders and his on the middle of her back. If either of them moved even a little…

Her head slowly moved from side to side. "Still not a good idea."

No kidding. She sounded less certain, though, and he didn't take his hands away. Neither did she.

This was reckless in so many ways, and although he completely agreed that it was a bad idea, part of him wondered how it would feel to kiss another woman after all these years. It was not as if he'd be cheating.

So what *would* he be doing? Scratching an itch? He slid one hand up Rory's back, deep beneath the long, soft strands of her hair. Her face tilted toward his, just enough to let him know she wouldn't stop him.

His mouth was practically on hers when he heard a key in the front door.

He and Rory shot apart. Too quickly.

"Ouch!" she said. "My hair."

The front door opened.

Her hair was snarled in his watch strap and he was madly trying to disentangle it when his mother walked in. Betsy halted just inside the room and at first she didn't say anything, then she grinned like someone who'd just been let in on a secret. "The play was great," she said, quickly regaining some of her usual composure. "It's been a long night, though. I'll just head upstairs. See you in the morning." She was halfway up the stairs and out of sight when she added, "Thanks for babysitting, Rory. *We* really appreciate it." Emphasis on *we*. He could picture that annoying smirk of hers.

Damn it. *This isn't what it looks like,* he wanted to yell after her.

Rory started to giggle.

Okay, it was *exactly* what it looked like, but it wasn't funny. "You have to hold still or I can't get us untangled."

She complied, but she didn't stop laughing. "I don't think I've ever had a guy's mother catch me making out with her son."

Making out? "I'm sure that's not what she thought was going on," he said, finally separating the two of them.

Laughter still brightened Rory's eyes. "Oh, I think that's exactly what she thought, and you were *so* going to kiss me."

True. And he very much regretted his mother's untimely arrival and the missed opportunity. He glanced at his watch and plucked a long blond hair from the strap. "It's getting late."

She leaned close and put her hands on his shoulders again. "It's not *too* late." She stood on her tiptoes and kissed him, full on the mouth, a lingering closed-mouth kiss that was both encouraging and a little disturbing.

Before he could respond, she backed away and smiled up at him. "Sleep well."

That was unlikely.

He went to bed, wishing like hell he could go upstairs

and take her into his arms. He ached for her. Not the usual physical ache a man felt for a woman, although he'd been feeling plenty of that. This was the kind of ache that started deep inside his chest and slowly filled it up until he had trouble breathing. He didn't just want to make love to her, although God knew he wanted to.

There. He'd admitted it, at least to himself.

What he really wanted, craved desperately, was to be with her *after* they'd made love. It had been more than a year since he'd experienced that kind of intimacy, that deep, personal connection with another human being that could only be achieved after physical and mutual satisfaction. And he wanted it badly.

Chapter Eight

Rory stretched and gazed up at the skylight. Although it was still early, the sky was starting to lighten and seemed to promise a beautiful day. She had crawled into bed last night expecting to toss and turn and relive the kiss, over and over again. Instead, sleep had been deep and satisfying. Maybe she needed to get kissed more often.

You kissed *him.*

That was true. She had. She had also flirted with him. Rather shamelessly, she had to admit. He was heart-stoppingly attractive, and it was pretty clear that he was just as attracted to her, but his response had been tentative. After her horrendous experience with Dean, tentative was good. Women must throw themselves at Mitch all the time, and yet he wasn't quick to reciprocate. That was definitely a point in his favor.

She snuggled under the covers and indulged in a slow-motion replay of last night's action. His lips might have been tentative, but those hands could work some serious magic. His fingers on her shoulders and neck, warming her skin…oh, my. He would be very good at making a woman feel oh-so-glad to be a woman. It would have been nice if he'd had a chance to spread some of that warmth around before Betsy had interrupted them.

Maybe she'd sworn off men for too long. How long had it been? Too long, obviously.

Not that there'd ever been a chance that her relationship with Dean was a forever kind of thing. He had been fun and charming, with a smooth working-his-way-up-the-corporate-ladder look about him, and he certainly knew his way around the bedroom. Of course, at the time, she hadn't realized just how extensive his experience had been.

Since then she'd had a few casual dinner dates, but not until last night had she let down her guard enough to take things to the next level. The next level being nothing more than a kiss, she reminded herself, and it hadn't been a date. Just a pleasant encounter between friends. Except she and Mitch weren't friends. They didn't even know each other, yet the sexual energy that sizzled between them was miles past friendly.

Mitch was completely different from Dean, or any other man she had dated. He was the strong, silent type who kept his emotions well in check. His wife's death had affected him profoundly, and according to Miranda, he found it difficult to talk about her, so although he wasn't married, he might as well be.

Her cell phone startled her out of the daydream. "Nicola, you had better not be calling me at this hour," she said, stumbling out of bed and grabbing her phone off the kitchen table. "Everything's under control and there will be no surprises. Not at the shower, and especially not on Jess's feet."

The call wasn't from Nic. It was Rory's father.

"Hi, Dad. How's the book tour going?"

"Exhausting, but good. I'll be glad to get home."

"Where are you now?"

"Dallas. Then Pittsburgh tomorrow and Boston on Wednesday. We'll be back in Manhattan on Thursday."

Talk about a brutal schedule. "How's Dayzee?"

He hesitated. "She seems fine," he said finally.

Oh, Dad, she thought. *Here we go again. Have you considered dating someone who's…oh, I don't know… your own age?* She didn't say it, though, and it's not like he hadn't heard it before. "She'll probably be glad to get home, too."

"Sorry we didn't get to spend much time together when I was in San Francisco, but it was good to see you."

"You, too." Rory climbed back into bed and pulled the covers up under her chin. Buick blinked sleepily from his usual spot at the foot of her bed.

"How's school?" he asked.

"I love teaching here. It feels as though I'm exactly where I'm meant to be."

"You were happy growing up in Mendocino, though, weren't you?"

It seemed like an odd question, and she didn't answer right away.

"Rory? Are you still there?"

"I'm here. Yes, I loved it up there, still do, but I prefer the city and this really feels like home."

"Glad to hear it. How's Mitch and that little girl of his?"

An even odder question. "Fine," she said cautiously. "Why do you ask?"

"He's a good man. Good father, too."

This was getting downright weird. Surely her father wasn't suggesting… Was he?

"I appreciate your observations, Dad, but I just met him and I don't think we have much in common." *Ha. You are such a liar. Before the phone rang, you were lying here thinking pretty much the same thing.*

"I've been thinking about what you said the last time we talked on the phone, that your mother and I were terrible role models in the getting-and-staying-married department."

"I didn't mean for you to take it so seriously."

"I didn't. Not until I saw you with Mitch and his daughter."

Huh? Exactly what had he seen?

"The two of you seem pretty interested in each other."

"Okay, who are you and where did you find my father's cell phone?"

Even his laughter sounded strangely serious. "I wish I could go back and redo things with your mother, set a proper example for you."

Rory didn't know what to say.

"You know I love your mother, right? Always have, always will. We just can't be together."

"Dad, that doesn't make sense."

"Yes, it does, Rory. God knows we've tried."

"If you love her that much, then what about all the girl-friends you've had since you got divorced?"

"Isn't it obvious?"

"Dad, this is me you're talking to. Your daughter. How could that be 'obvious'?"

"I knew I'd never find another woman like your mother, so I've never tried."

Sam Borland's self-psychoanalysis actually made sense. Sort of. "You've dated a string of woman half your age with whom you have nothing in common because you're still in love with Mom?"

"It's taken me a while to figure it out, but yeah, that seems to be what I've been doing."

"And exactly when did you figure this out?"

"At the art gallery."

Talk about being blindsided. "Have you shared this with her?"

"Some things are best left alone."

"She deserves to hear this, Dad." And part of her—the inner-little-girl part—wanted him to tell her mother because that part of her had always secretly hoped her parents would find happiness together.

"I'm telling you this because I don't want my mistakes to affect your happiness, not to get your hopes up."

So after all these years, her hopes had been that obvious? "I still think you should tell her."

"I'll think about it. For now, though, can we keep this between us?"

"Of course." There were lots of things she could discuss openly with her mother, but this was not one of them.

"And you'll give Mitch a chance?" She could tell he was smiling when he asked that.

"Okay, now you're pushing your luck."

They both laughed, and he sounded as relieved as she was to change the subject.

"What are you doing today?" he asked.

"Shoe-shopping with Jess. She needs something to wear to Nic's wedding."

"That sounds like fun."

She groaned. "Easy for you to say. You've never had to wrestle her out of her sneakers and into a pair of heels."

Her father chuckled. "How is Jess?" He liked all of her friends, but he'd always had a real soft spot for Jess—said she reminded him of the son he'd never had. If anyone else said that, tomboy Jess would deck them, but when it came to Rory's dad, she'd often said he was like the father she'd always wished she'd had.

"She's the same as ever. Struggling to make ends meet and refusing to let anyone give her a hand."

"Say hi to her for me."

"I will."

"Looks like our cab is here, sugar. I have to run."

"Thanks for calling, Dad. I love you."

"Love you, too, Rory." And then he was gone.

She disconnected and dropped the phone onto the bed beside her, then stretched her arms overhead and yawned. Buick rolled onto his side and did the same. "Good morning, lazy-bones," she said to him. "This is going to be a good day." He lay there motionless, as if in silent agreement.

She was lounging in bed, watching the sky lighten while mulling over her father's bombshell, when she heard voices below. Miranda's, then Mitch's. Last night she'd figured out that his bedroom must be at the front of the house, which meant it was right below hers.

She listened closely and heard Miranda's laughter. Mitch was a good father and a good man, but so was her father. If Sam's unexpected confession was intended to make her look at life a little differently, it was working. She wasn't ready to rush into anything, but the thought of exploring a relationship, maybe even one with Mitch, was not such a bad idea. She rolled over and crawled out of bed. Shoe-shopping with Jess was a whole other matter.

MIRANDA BURST INTO THE front foyer ahead of her father just as Rory was coming downstairs.

"Miss Sunshine! Me and my dad are going to the school so I can practice hopscotching." Miranda was dressed in a pair of jeans with faded knees, pink sneakers and a light blue jacket with too-short sleeves, and her curls had been gathered into two adorable pigtails. Rory wondered if Mitch had done her hair.

He waited while she and Miranda went down the steps to the sidewalk, then followed them.

"That sounds like a fun way to spend a Saturday morning. You can teach your dad how to play hopscotch, too."

She grinned at him. He didn't smile back. He looked tired, as though he hadn't slept well, and he seemed even more withdrawn than usual. Surely not because of last night?

"Watch this." Miranda demonstrated her hopscotch jumps up the sidewalk, spun around in mid-jump, and hopped back down. "Do you wanna come with us?"

Yes, she did. "Sounds like fun, but a friend and I are going shopping."

The little girl stopped jumping. "Can I come up and play with Buick when you get back?"

"Miranda, you can't invite yourself to someone else's house."

"But it's our house, too."

Rory laughed and tweaked one of Miranda's pigtails. "Have fun at the school," she said, keeping her gaze connected with Mitch's. "And I meant what I said about showing your dad how to hopscotch. Even grown-ups need to have some fun once in a while."

He didn't exactly smile, but the creases at the corners of his mouth deepened a little.

All right, she thought. *That's more like it.* As she walked around the front of her van, she watched them walk hand-in-hand up the hill to Haight Street. Miranda's free hand swung back and forth, and Rory found herself wishing she was holding it.

What are you thinking?

Mitch glanced over his shoulder. She gave him a finger wave, and he finally smiled for real.

Oh, yeah. She was thinking the same thing he was thinking.

She unlocked the door and tossed her bag on Vanna's passenger seat as she climbed behind the wheel.

The van sputtered to life. She slipped it into gear, released the hand brake and checked the side mirror just in time to see Mitch and his daughter disappear around the corner. As she pulled away from the curb, shopping for shoes suddenly seemed like an excellent idea. Jess would find suitable shoes to wear to the wedding if it killed her. Rory would find a pair, too. The kind of shoes that would really make Mitch smile when she found the right opportunity to wear them.

RORY PUSHED THE BUZZER at the front door of Jess's apartment building. Her friend lived in the South of Market area, about six blocks from The Whiskey Sour. The bar was in the part of SoMa that was undergoing rejuvenation. Her apartment was not.

"Hang on. I'll be right down."

"No way," Rory said. "I'm coming up."

"Why do you want to come up? We're going shopping. Besides, my place is a mess."

"You're wasting time. Let me in."

"If you're in such a hurry, we should get going."

"Jess—" Rory knew her well enough to know she was likely wearing a baggy shirt and an old pair of jeans.

"Fine." The abrupt release of the lock on the front door matched the clipped tone of Jess's voice on the intercom.

Rory smiled as she pushed the door open and dashed up one flight of stairs to the second floor. She tapped on her friend's door, and it flew open.

The place was as neat as a pin, but the same couldn't be said for Jess. She had on her trademark discount-store jeans, a yellow T-shirt and a man's once-white dress shirt, worn jacket-style with the sleeves rolled up to the elbows.

"I knew it," Rory said.

"What?"

"You can't try on wedding shoes when you're dressed for a game of touch football."

"I dress like this all the time."

"I know."

"To each her own. Not everyone has a closet full of funky clothes."

Rory laughed. "I'll take that as a compliment, but you know that kind of sweet talk won't work on me." She assessed her friend's worn sneakers and the wrinkled shirt. "You need a pair of shoes to go with a bridesmaid dress, not for schlepping around behind the bar."

"It's one night. What difference does it make?"

If one approach didn't work, try another, or so her father always said. Too bad he was better at dishing out advice than he was at following it. "Think of it this way," Rory said. "It could be good for business."

Jess's eyes narrowed, but she relaxed her hands-on-hips stance. "How's that?"

"Think of all the people who'll be at the reception. Other business owners, potential customers. It'll be a good opportunity to—" She stopped herself before she said *schmooze*. Jess was *so* not a schmoozer. "To talk to other business people, have them take you seriously, get some ideas on how to build a clientele."

"And I need shoes for that?"

"If you want to kick butt, you need to dress for success. Now go put on a pair of sandals and a skirt. You do own a skirt?"

"Yeah, but I haven't worn it in a couple of years. It might not fit."

It? She shouldn't be surprised that Jess's wardrobe included only one skirt. Fortunately, in all the years she'd known her, Jess's weight hadn't fluctuated more than a few ounces. "Go put it on. We won't recognize the perfect shoes with blue jeans bunched around your ankles."

Jess rolled her eyes.

Rory pointed to her bedroom. "No more arguments. Hurry up and change so we can get going."

"Anyone ever tell you that you sound *exactly* like your mother when you get all bossy like this?" Jess asked as she disappeared into the bedroom.

Yes, she'd heard it. More than once. Maybe that was why she had so much trouble with relationships.

In less than two minutes Jess was back. The jeans had been replaced by a knee-length denim skirt, the sneakers with a pair of black flip-flops. The yellow T-shirt worked but the man-shirt didn't.

Pick your battles, Rory thought. *That* was always her mother's advice, and if anyone knew how to pick a battle, it was her mother.

"Where are we going?" Jess asked once they were in the van and underway.

"Downtown. A couple of my favorite shoe stores are having great sales right now."

"A downtown shoe store doesn't sound like a place I can afford."

"If we don't find anything there, we'll check the department stores." There was no point in reminding her that Nicola had offered to pay for the shoes, because Jess had flatly refused. No handouts for her.

"I also have a surprise for you." If she told her about the pedicure, Jess would come up with a million excuses not to go. For the same reason, Rory had also decided it was best not to mention lingerie until they were actually in the store.

"Am I going to like this surprise?"

Rory stopped at a red light. "Who doesn't love a surprise?"

"Remember what Nic said about her shower? She doesn't like surprises, and neither do I."

Rory laughed. "Right. You and Nic are like two peas in a pod."

Jess leaned back in her seat and laughed, too. Of the five of them, Nicola and Jess were polar opposites. "Okay, fine. Surprise me."

The light turned green and, as Rory eased off the clutch, the van lurched into the intersection.

"I think Vanna needs a new clutch," Rory said.

"I think Rory needs a new van." Jess hastily patted the dashboard. "No offense."

"We both know you didn't mean it."

"So, other than planning to torture me today, what else have you been up to?"

Where to start? Looking after Miranda? Kissing Mitch? She wasn't ready to talk about either. The phone call from her father? *That* she needed to talk about, and Jess was not only a good listener, she kept things to herself.

"My dad called this morning. He says hello."

"Cool. I'm sorry I missed him when he was in town. How is he?"

"To be honest, I'm not sure. I mean, he seemed fine when he was here, but we had a weird conversation this morning."

"In what way?"

"I told you that he came to the opening of my mother's art exhibit, didn't I?" Rory turned on the left-turn signal, remembered that it wasn't working, and quickly rolled down the window and stuck out her arm.

"With the ditzy girlfriend. You mentioned it when you called to remind me we were going shopping."

"I didn't say she was ditzy."

"Was she?"

Rory sighed. Dayzee had seemed more scatterbrained than most. "I'm afraid so."

"No offense, but your dad's girlfriends are *always* ditzy."

"I know. That's not what his phone call was about, though. Not really. He told me…" A little thrill of antici-pation shivered through her. She'd given up any hope of her parents reconciling years ago. Rekindling that dream now would be childish, foolish.

"What? What did he say?"

"He's still in love with my mother."

Jess's exhale came out as long, low whistle. "Wow. He told you that?"

Rory geared down as she slowed for another red light. "Yes."

"Wow. Out of the blue, your father unloads that juicy bit of info. How did your mother react?"

"He asked me not to say anything to her."

"Okay, that *is* weird. Why tell you and not your mother?"

Good question. "He thinks he's responsible for my attitude about marriage and kids."

"From everything you've told me, he kind of is. He and your mom, that is."

Jess was right, but it didn't seem fair to unload all the blame on them. "Marriage isn't for everyone. I'm perfectly happy, I have a job I love, great friends, I get to spend my summers traveling."

"But?"

"There's no but."

"Oh, yes, there is. Something must be going on for your dad to suddenly be all worried about you and confessing that he's still in love with your mom after all this time."

Rory pretended to concentrate on driving. "Man, there's a lot of traffic, even for a Saturday."

"So, I'm right."

"About what?"

"About whatever it is that's got your dad wanting you to reconsider your aversion to long-term relationships. Spill it."

How much could she say without giving Jess the wrong idea about her and Mitch? "I invited my landlady and her son—"

"The super-hot firefighter?"

Rory shot her a quick warning glance.

"Keep talking. I'm listening. Just think of me as your favorite friendly bartender. Kind of like a shrink, only free." Jess grinned and made a zipping motion across her mouth.

"My landlady, her son and his little girl came to my mom's opening at the gallery. My dad seems to think something's going on between us."

"Between you and the super-hot… Sorry. Between you and the firefighter?"

Rory pulled into a parking garage and maneuvered the van into a spot. "His name is Mitch."

"Is your dad right?"

"No." Not really.

"Ha. I don't believe you."

"Why not?" Rory took the keys out of the ignition and stowed them in her handbag.

Jess's scrutiny was intense. "Have you seen Mitch since the gallery?"

Rory felt her face go warm.

"So something *is* going on."

"Nothing's going on. I looked after Miranda—his daughter—last night. That's all."

"You're babysitting for this guy?"

"No. Not for him. He wasn't home and his mother had to go out, so she asked me to keep an eye on her."

"Who came home first?"

Rory's face heated up some more. Damn. "What do you mean?"

"Were you still there when he came home?"

"What does that have to do with anything?"

Jess laughed. "There's my answer, and here's my diagnosis. Your dad's right. You've got it bad, girl."

Rory gave up. "I do not. But you'll keep this between us, right?"

Her friend feigned innocence. "You *don't* want me to tell the girls there's *nothing* going on between you and Mitch?"

Even Rory had to laugh at that. "Don't tell them anything. Please?"

Jess leaned across the van and gave her a hug. "Your secret's safe with me. That's what friends are for."

"That, and shopping." She grinned, knowing she could count on Jess to keep this under her hat, at least until she figured out what *this* was.

THE PLAYGROUND BEHIND the school was empty. Not surprising, this early on a Saturday morning.

"Do you have a quarter, Dad? We need a quarter for a marker."

He dug some change out of his pocket. "Why does it have to be a quarter?"

"'Cause Miss Sunshine says."

Right. Miss Sunshine had made a mighty big impact for someone who had just come into their lives. Last night he had lain awake a long time, going back over that kiss—and over it, and over it—alternately wishing it hadn't stopped at one and then reprimanding himself for letting it happen at all.

He handed a quarter to Miranda, who had already positioned herself at one end of the white-painted hopscotch court, and took a few steps back.

"This is what you have to do," she said. "Throw the quarter in the first square and stand on one foot, like this." She demonstrated the stance and looked up at him as though checking to make sure he was paying attention.

"Got it," he said.

"You have to jump over top of the square with the quarter in it and land in the next one." She landed on her right foot, arms stretched like a pair of wings and body teetering till she regained her balance. "See?"

"I do."

"Then you get to jump on both feet." She demonstrated that move with more precision, landing with both feet on squares three and four. "That's the easiest one."

She explained the moves as though she expected him to take a turn. Did she? Laura would have joined in without a second thought, leaving him to watch from the sidelines. There was a time when Miranda would have been happy with that.

She hopped on the remaining squares on one foot, landed on both feet in the semi-circle at the other end, and started the return trip. She stopped when she reached the second-to-last square. "Now you got to stay on one foot, pick up the quarter and jump out. But you still can't jump on that square, even though the quarter's gone," she advised as she leaped off the court. "See? I did it!"

"Yes, you did. I'll bet you've been practicing at recess."

"Yup. Me and Ashley play all the time." She held out the quarter. "Your turn."

"Oh, I don't know…" He opened his hand and reluctantly accepted the coin. "I don't think dads are very good at this sort of thing."

"Miss Sunshine said."

Yes, she had. And Miss Sunshine had known full well that Miranda would expect him to give this a shot. He cast a self-conscious glance over one shoulder and then the other. What the hell. One attempt at hopscotch wouldn't kill him.

He dropped the quarter into the first square and landed on one foot in the next square, flailed for a second and quickly hopped on both feet into the next two squares. This was harder than it looked.

Miranda stood outside the painted lines and laughed. "You're doing good." She sounded like a miniature school-teacher.

Should he remind her that she should say "doing well"?

No.

She was enjoying being the one in charge for a change. He should concentrate on finishing the game of hopscotch and save the grammar lesson for another time.

The hardest part was picking up the quarter at the end. Standing on one foot, reaching down to the ground, picking up a quarter and *not* falling flat on his face wasn't easy for a guy who was over six feet and not that graceful to start with.

"See? It's fun."

She was right. It kind of was. Especially now that it was over—except it wasn't.

"Now it's my turn again." She took the quarter from him and carefully tossed it into the second square. "We have to do this for all the squares. Three and four are the hardest 'cause you don't get to land on both feet at once."

By the third round he stopped feeling like a bull in a china shop and was happy to let her win, although he quickly realized that was a given anyway. If he stepped on a line, he lost his turn. If the quarter bounced out of the square, he lost his turn. And he did both several times, never intentionally.

"You're way better at this than I am," he said.

"I'm better than Ashley, too. Miss Sunshine says 'practice makes perfect' so I've been practicing lots."

Miranda won the game handily and, as he offered her a congratulatory handshake, he noticed they had attracted a small audience. A young mother and her two kids—both younger than Miranda—were watching from the sidewalk on the other side of the chain-link fence. He wasn't crazy about having people watch his clumsy attempt at a childhood game, but he didn't feel as embarrassed as he would have half an hour ago.

"Here's your quarter, Dad."

"Why don't you keep it? You can put it in your piggy bank when we get home."

"'Kay. Thanks!" She tucked the coin in her pocket, and then she waved at the family on the sidewalk. "That's Kayla. She's in first grade. And that's her mom and her little sister."

They all waved back and, to Mitch's relief, continued on their way. Being seen playing hopscotch was one thing. Having a conversation about it was a whole other story.

They walked toward the gate and Miranda tucked her hand in his. "I have lots of money in my bank."

"Do you have a job I don't know about?" he teased.

She giggled. "No. I've got all my tooth fairy money, and Grams gives me her change whenever we go to the store."

"Are you saving up for something?"

Her head bobbed up and down. "Lots of stuff. I want new shoes, the kind that have wheels in them, and a bike and some nail polish like Miss Sunshine wears."

He could think of so many reasons why that was not a good idea.

"Last night when we read *Cinderella,* she said I can go upstairs to her place and we'll have tea. A real tea party, with cake and ice cream and everything."

It sounded as if he needed to have a talk with Rory. It was one thing to lead him on, but not his daughter. She'd made it clear she didn't want a family, and lately Miranda had made several references to having a mother. A mother who knew how to play hopscotch, like Miss Sunshine.

Miranda had already lost her real mother. He would not stand by and watch her have her hopes dashed by a breezy woman in brightly colored clothes and even more brightly colored toe polish. A woman who had unabashedly kissed him last night, and given him a saucy little finger wave that morning before driving away in that outrageously painted van.

"Do you want to have tea with us?"

"We'll see."

"When you say that, it means no."

"It means I'll think about it." And then yes, once he'd come up with a decent-sounding reason, he would say no.

"Can we go for ice cream today?"

"Sure."

"At Fisherman's Wharf?"

"Not this time, princess." Laura had always said that too much of a good thing spoiled the fun.

"So no cable-car ride either?"

"Not today."

She didn't ask why and he was grateful for that, but he knew it would come up again sooner or later. Probably sooner. "We'll find a good place for ice cream, though."

They turned the corner onto their street, and the first thing he noticed was that Rory's van was not parked in front of the house. Not that he expected to see it—she had already told them she was spending the day with a friend—but it was always the first thing he looked for when he came home, and that bugged him.

FOUR HOURS LATER, Rory, Jess and an assortment of shopping bags were back in the van.

"Do you want me to drop you off at the bar?"

"I can't go to work in a skirt. I have to go home first."

"It'll be a shame to cover up those gorgeous feet."

Jess had strenuously argued against red toe polish, but Rory had insisted. It was a perfect match for her new retro-looking blue shoes with the shiny red high heels and little red bows above the open toes. They were on sale and Rory had briefly debated buying herself a pair, but then she'd spotted the strappy, stiletto wonders—entirely studded with sparkly rhinestones, more like jewelry than shoes—and had completely blown her budget for the rest of the month. Perfect for the wedding, and just the thing to take the starch out of a certain uptight super-hot single dad's collar.

"Can you picture me changing a keg in flip-flops and a skirt?"

"I can't picture it at all," Rory said, laughing, "but that's a good point. You can always wear your new undies under your jeans and T-shirt."

Jess rose to the bait. "I can't believe I let you talk me into spending that much money on a bra and panties no one will ever see."

"You never know…" They had found a strapless bra and matching boyshorts in a shade of blue almost identical to the dresses. Perfect for Jess, and almost certain to knock some guy's socks off.

"I'm not going to pick up some guy at the wedding and show him my underwear, but I think we know who's going to see yours."

"Ha-ha." Rory had bought the shoes with Mitch in mind and, let's admit it, he had also crossed her mind when she'd chosen the bra and the cheeky pair of panties in soft baby blue. "He won't even be at the wedding."

"He, who?" Jess's question sounded casual and completely innocent.

Rory knew better than to respond, but that didn't mean her friend was prepared to drop it.

"Maybe the father of the little girl you bought the jacket for?"

Choosing the bright yellow windbreaker had seemed like a good idea at the time. Miranda loved that color, and the jacket she'd had on this morning was way too small. But as soon as Rory had paid for it, and especially after she saw Jess's reaction, she knew it was a bad idea. Mitch would almost certainly disapprove, and Jess would never let it go. "He's busy and probably doesn't like to shop. I'm just trying to help."

She knew that wasn't true, and so did Jess. "Are you sure that being a stand-in mom is the best way to go about this?"

"I am not a stand-in anything. I'm just a friend trying to help out."

"And I think the lady protests too much. You always said you wanted a traditional family. This could be it."

"I used to wish *my* family had been more traditional. I never said I was going to start one of my own."

"I guess we'll have to wait and see." Jess sounded like she already knew what the result would be, and although she couldn't be more wrong, for once Rory was happy to let her have the last word.

Chapter Nine

On Thursday during afternoon recess, Rory went down the hall to get drawing paper from the supply room. Her students usually worked on a social studies project for the last part of the day, but they were a fractious bunch today and she had decided a quiet art activity might help to settle them down. She had the makings of a headache, and after lunch she'd even lost her patience and raised her voice at them. Today was one of those rare days when she looked forward to getting out of the classroom.

She'd had a lot on her mind since her Friday-night encounter with Mitch and the next day's phone call from her father. She hadn't seen Mitch since Saturday morning, and if she had to guess, she'd say he was avoiding her. The phone call from her father had left her feeling rattled, and Jess's suggestion that Rory wasn't just falling for Mitch, she was also falling for his daughter, was completely ridiculous. She wasn't looking for a family or a relationship with a man who had one. None of this explained her impulsive behavior on Friday night, or why she'd bought a new jacket for Miranda. It was still in the bag in the back of her van because after Jess's suggestion that she wanted to be Mitch's stand-in wife, she had decided to return it. Added to all that, Nicola was calling several times a day to discuss wedding arrangements, and now Nic's mother had started calling about the bridal shower.

After school today, she would put all of them on the back burner and they could darned well sit there and simmer. She would go home, turn off her cell phone, take something for her headache and curl up and have a nap with Buick. As she walked past the office on her way back to her classroom, Shirley, the school secretary, waved a couple of message slips at her. "You have a message from Miranda Donovan's grandmother. And one from your friend Nicola's mother."

Rory squinted at the notes, trying to decipher the woman's spidery scrawl.

The first was from Betsy. *Repair man coming this afternoon. Wants to know if you can bring Miranda home after school.* No problem, since she was going straight home anyway.

The second was from Nicola's mother. *Pick up supplies for bridal shower at the rental store and drop them off at Nic's mother's place.* The word *please,* clearly an afterthought, had been scrawled sideways in the margin at the beginning of the sentence. Okay. Not going straight home.

"Thanks," Rory said. "I'll call them."

"How's that working out?" Shirley asked. "Living with Miranda's family?" She'd been the school's secretary since Mitch had been a student here, and she had one finger firmly on the pulse of the school and everyone associated with it. Which was mostly a good thing, except when it got personal.

"Um…" *How does she know about that?* Rory wondered. "I'm just renting an apartment from them." Shirley's cryptic smile acknowledged her explanation but implied that she was waiting for an answer, making Rory feel like a child who'd been sent to the principal's office. "It's working out really well. Thanks for asking." She beat a hasty retreat before the woman could ask any more questions.

The big clock on the back wall showed that recess would be over in five minutes. She fished her cell phone out of her bag and called Nicola's mother to learn that she had rented decorations for Nic's shower. The store couldn't deliver them till Saturday and she needed them *now,* even though the shower was three days away. Besides, she was sure everything would fit in Rory's van.

Rory searched in vain for a bottle of aspirin while she dialed Betsy's number. Betsy answered on the first ring. "Sorry to ask for another favor so soon, but Mitch is working today and I have someone coming to check the wiring on the kiln. He couldn't say exactly when he'll be here and when he does show up, I'll be down in my studio with him. Would you mind bringing Miranda home and keeping an eye on her till I'm through?"

"Um, sure. I'm organizing a shower for a friend and have to run some errands after school. Is it okay if I take Miranda with me?"

"Of course. I'm sure she'll be thrilled to go with you."

The bell rang to end recess and her students stampeded into the classroom. Only one more hour to go, she told herself.

RORY UNLOCKED THE passenger door of her van.

"Goody!" Miranda climbed into the passenger seat. "In our car I have to sit in a booster seat in the back. Dad says it's 'cause of the air bags."

Hm. Vanna didn't have a backseat, but she didn't have air bags, either. "Will you be okay up here?"

"Yup." She leaned around the seat so she could look into the back. "I've never ridden in a van that has a kitchen," she said as Rory slid behind the steering wheel. "That's *so* cool."

The way she said "*so* cool" was an amusing contrast to the little girl who still needed a booster seat.

"I like to travel in the summertime when there's no school." She turned the key in the ignition and the engine sputtered to life. "The van is great because I have a place to sleep and to cook meals."

"What about Buick?"

"Sometimes he comes with me—he likes riding in the van—and sometimes he stays with my mother in Mendocino." Copper jokingly referred to him as her grand-cat. Rory released the hand brake. "Do up your seat belt, okay?"

"'Kay."

Rory waited till she heard the buckle click, then pulled out of the parking space.

"I wish me and Dad had a van so we could go places."

"Where would you like to go?" Rory asked, maneuvering into traffic.

The little girl didn't need to give that any thought. "Disneyland. Ashley went this summer and she got Mickey Mouse ears."

"Does your dad know that's where you'd like to go?" Rory asked. Miranda didn't hesitate to speak up at school, but she seemed cautious about what she said to her father. It was interesting that she was as protective of him as he was of her.

"Yup. He said we'll go when I'm older."

"I see."

"How come you painted flowers on your van?"

"My mother painted them," Rory explained. "It used to be her van, and she likes flowers and bright colors." And because her mother used to be a hippie and that was what hippies did. She could imagine Miranda asking what a hippie was and it would be too tempting to tell her that her grandmother was one. "Did I tell you my van has a name?"

"Nuh-uh. What it is?"

"Vanna White."

Miranda giggled. "She's the lady on TV."

"And she has the same initials as my Volkswagen. VW."

"That's funny. Me and Dad should think up a name for our car."

Mitch drove a new but nondescript-looking SUV. Not the kind of vehicle that inspired a name, but she decided to play along with Miranda. "What's your favorite name?" she asked.

Miranda answered without hesitation. "Laura."

Hm. That had been her mother's name, and Rory was absolutely certain that never in a million years would Mitch go along with naming his car after her.

"But I think ours is a boy car," Miranda said before Rory could come up with a response.

"Really? Why do you think that?"

"'Cause it's blue, and 'cause it's very big and strong."

Interesting observation. Rory suspected it had every safety device ever invented, which was likely why Mitch had chosen it, and the dark blue color reminded her of a police uniform. "How about Inspector Gadget?"

Miranda's laughter bubbled through the van. "That's a good name! I'll tell my dad that's what we should call it."

Rory tried to imagine Mitch's reaction. He'd almost certainly humor his daughter, but she doubted he'd ever call a car anything but a car.

After circling the block twice, Rory finally spotted the rental store in a little strip mall. "You should put on your jacket," Rory said after she parked the van and pocketed her keys. The sun had dipped well to the west and the temperature had dropped accordingly.

Miranda unzipped her backpack. "Oh, no. I must've left it in my cubby at school." She started to shiver as soon as she clambered out of the van. "Brrr."

There's the jacket you bought on Saturday, Rory reminded herself. She would have to remove the tags, which meant she wouldn't be able to return it after all, but she couldn't let the little girl get chilled. "Try this on," she said, pulling the jacket out of the bag.

"How come you have a kid's jacket?"

"Oh. Well, I was planning to give it to my friend's daughter."

Liar.

"For her birthday. Which is next week."

Liar.

"Is she going to come to visit you?" Miranda sounded hopeful about the possibility of a visitor her age.

"No. She lives in Mendocino," Rory said, naming the first city that popped into her head. "I was planning to mail it to her."

Pants on fire.

Rory held the yellow windbreaker so Miranda could slip her arms into the flannel-lined sleeves.

"It's nice and warm."

"And it fits, too." She dug a pair of nail clippers out of her purse and snipped the tag off the sleeve. "There you go. You can keep this one and I'll get another one for my friend. My friend's daughter." Better keep her story straight, especially if she expected Mitch to accept her explanation. She zipped the jacket. "How's that?"

"Good. I like yellow and my old one is getting too small."

As they walked across the parking lot, Rory felt a small, warm hand slip into hers. She squeezed the little hand, looked down into a pair of trusting blue eyes, and she was done for. Scattered snippets of the conversations she'd had with her friends and her father raced through her mind.

Love doesn't have to be complicated.

Give Mitch a chance.

He's a good man. A good father.

You always said you wanted a traditional family.

It's way too complicated, and I don't do complicated.

Being with Miranda felt gratifying, natural, simple. Not complicated at all. *Watch your step,* Rory warned herself.

The store's showroom was filled with displays of every kind of wedding paraphernalia a bride could possibly want, and a lot of things most would never dream of.

A tall, dark-haired woman greeted them from behind the counter. "How can I help you?"

"I'm here to pick up decorations for a friend's bridal shower." She gave the woman Nicola's name and waited while she looked it up on the computer.

Miranda let go of her hand and wandered inside a miniature gazebo draped with white netting. "Look! It's like Cinderella lives here."

"Here it is. Everything is ready to go." The clerk pointed to a small mountain of boxes stacked by the door. "We even had enough centerpieces in stock."

Centerpieces? For a bridal shower? She still thought an evening at Jess's bar would have been just as much fun and a lot less trouble, but Nic's mom was doing most of the work and footing the entire bill. She had hired a caterer so Rory didn't have to shop for food, and Paige was looking after the shower gift from the four bridesmaids.

"We have a loading zone right here in front of the store. Will this fit in your car?"

"I have a van. I'm sure everything will fit."

"Very good. If you'd like to leave your daughter here while you move your van, I'll keep an eye on her."

"Excuse me?"

"Your daughter," she repeated, gesturing toward the gazebo.

"Oh." She should explain that Miranda was not her daughter. For some reason, she didn't. "Thanks, but I'll take her with me. Miranda? Let's go get the van, then you can help me load the boxes."

"'Kay. I'm pretending I'm a princess and this is my castle. Will there be one of these at the wedding?"

She sincerely hoped not.

It was nearly five o'clock when they left the wedding store and headed for Cow Hollow. After not wanting to spend another minute with the children in her classroom, she had just pretended to be the mother of one of them. The crazy emotions brought on by holding Miranda's hand should have passed by now.

They hadn't.

For the second Friday night in a row, Rory was spending the evening at home. She really needed to get a life. At least a social one. She lounged on the sofa with Buick curled up by her feet and surfed through several channels on TV, stopping at a news broadcast that was reporting on a fire that had happened late last night. Mitch had worked last night. Not that it mattered one way or the other, but she had fallen into the habit of figuring out when he worked and when he had days off.

On the television, the flames shooting from the roof of the house seemed impervious to the water gushing from an aerial hose. She leaned closer as the camera showed a close-up of one truck. It was from Mitch's station. Three people—a woman and her two children—were being examined by paramedics. There was a brief interview with a neighbor, who told the reporter they were the only residents of the house, so it seemed likely that no one was trapped inside. Then the camera cut to an image of a firefighter carrying a shivering, terrified-looking little dog wrapped in a blanket.

"Aw, they even rescued the dog." She gave Buick a gentle scruff behind the ears. He stood up and glowered at her for disturbing him, then stretched out his front legs, butt in the air, and flopped onto his other side.

Rory's cell phone rang and Nicola's name appeared on the call display. *Oh, for heaven's sake. What now?*

The shower was under control.

Jess had appropriate shoes.

Appointments for the bridesmaids' hair and makeup had been made.

And yes, a new wristwatch seemed like an appropriate wedding gift for Jonathan. Actually, she had no clue whether it was or not, but Nicola didn't need to know that.

She answered this call reluctantly. "Hi, Nic. What's up?"

"You won't believe this."

No, she probably wouldn't.

"One of Jonathan's groomsmen broke his leg yesterday."

The guy had some nerve. Rory would have laughed if she didn't feel so sorry him. "How did that happen?"

"He was cleaning the gutters on his house and his ladder slipped."

"Ouch. Poor guy."

"Don't get me wrong," Nicola said. "I feel terrible for him, but I wish he could have waited till after the wedding. There's no way he can get his tux over the cast, and I *so* don't want a man on crutches in my wedding photos."

That did make her laugh. "Sweetie, I'm pretty sure he didn't do this on purpose."

Nic laughed, too. "I know I'm obsessing about everything, and you've been *so* patient with me. I just want my day to be perfect. And I wasn't really calling to complain about Greg's broken leg because I've already found a solution."

No surprise there. Nicola was a natural-born problem-solver. Rory just didn't understand why she had to be filled in on every minute detail.

"That's good."

"We're asking Mitch to fill in."

Had she heard that correctly? "What?"

"Jonathan knows him, and Jess said the two of you kind of have a thing going on and that you and his family have hit it off, so it seemed like the obvious thing to do."

Jess, you are going to pay for this. "She shouldn't have told you about that."

"Why not?"

"That was a private conversation, and it's not like it sounds. Mitch and I do *not* have a 'thing.'"

Nicola's laugh bubbled through the phone. "Don't get all defensive with me. We're all friends so there shouldn't be any secrets. He and Jonathan are friends, and you didn't have a date for the wedding, so it was the perfect solution to everyone's problem."

Who said I had a problem? "I don't know, Nic. What if he thinks I put you up to this?"

"He won't think that. Besides, Jon has already asked him and he said he'd do it. I'm just calling to let you know it's all set. I have to run. I still have a million things to do, but I'll see you at my shower on Sunday."

Rory snapped her phone shut and tossed it onto the coffee table. In spite of her misgivings, she still felt a little sizzle of anticipation. She and Mitch would get to spend the whole day together, dance together and she wouldn't have to find another occasion to dazzle him with the shoes.

Chapter Ten

After fighting a house fire most of the night, Mitch had come home exhausted and slept for a good part of the day. He was thankful that his mother had taken Miranda to school and brought her home. Before he went downstairs, he checked the street from his bedroom window. Rory's van was parked in its usual spot in front of the house.

He had given up telling himself it was none of his business, especially after getting a phone call from one of the guys on his basketball team. Jon was marrying a friend of Rory's and he needed a last-minute stand-in for a groomsman who had fallen off a ladder and broken his leg. Thanks to that guy's rotten luck, Mitch would get to spend an entire evening with Rory. He hadn't been looking for a reason to do that, but he wasn't going to pass up the opportunity.

The kitchen smelled great. His mother was taking a meat loaf out of the oven and Miranda was setting the table.

"How was school today?"

"Me and Ashley played hopscotch at recess and I won, and today was Matthew's birthday and his mom brought cupcakes, and Miss Sunshine read us a book about weather and I learned how to spell evaporate. *E-v-a-p-o-r-a-t-e*, evaporate."

"You had a busy day!" He picked her up and hugged her, finding as he always did an overwhelming sense of love and obligation as he felt those warm, trusting little arms wrap around his neck.

"Yesterday after school I went shopping with Miss Sunshine."

"Did you?" He gave his mother a questioning look.

"I had someone come to look at the kiln. He was still here when school was dismissed, so I asked Rory to bring her home."

"Miss Sunshine went shopping for stuff for her friend's wedding, so I went with her and she gave me a new jacket. It's yellow."

Mitch set her down. Why would Rory give clothing to his daughter?

His mother's explanation alleviated his concern. "Miranda left her jacket at school and Rory had one that she'd bought as a gift for someone."

"Then we should give it back."

That earned him a warning look from his mother.

"She said I can keep it," Miranda said in a matter-of-fact tone. "Grams, which side does the fork go on?"

"Left side." His mother drained a pot of potatoes. "Would you like to help me mash these?"

"Yup. I'll get the milk."

As far as these two were concerned, the discussion about the jacket was over. Not for him. After dinner he'd go up to Rory's and pay her for it.

AFTER DINNER MITCH helped his mother clean up the kitchen while Miranda went upstairs to brush her teeth and pick out a bedtime story. Last Friday night he'd played basketball with his friends, but tonight he decided to stay home. He'd tuck his daughter in for the night, and then he'd deal with the matter of Rory's unexpected gift.

"That was a good dinner," he said to his mother. "Thanks."

"You're welcome. We haven't had meat loaf in a while and it was always one of your favorites," she said as she wiped the table. "I'm sorry about asking Rory to look after Miranda again, but I haven't been able to get the timer on the kiln to work properly and I know she doesn't mind."

He was tempted to say *he* minded, but that would sound petty and wasn't entirely true. What he minded was the ease with which she seemed to be fitting into their lives, and the amount of time he spent thinking about her. Should he mention the wedding?

His mother crossed the kitchen to the sink and rinsed the dishcloth. "The two of you seem to be hitting it off."

She hadn't said anything about walking in on them last Friday night, but he knew better than to think the subject was forgotten. He decided to hold off on telling her about the wedding. "What you saw the other night wasn't what it looked like."

The look she gave him was one he hadn't seen since he was a teenager. There was no fooling her, so why even bother trying? He wasn't a kid, he didn't need to explain himself, and when he stumbled upon a woman sleeping on his sofa, he shouldn't feel guilty about kissing her.

"Are we done here?" he asked. "I should run up and check on Miranda."

"Off you go. I can manage."

He took the stairs two at a time. Half an hour later his daughter was tucked in and he was standing in the foyer staring up the staircase that led to Rory's apartment. He hadn't been up there since he'd helped her move in.

After a couple of light taps on the door, he heard her get up and walk across the apartment. He let out his breath, realizing he'd been holding it.

Rory opened the door and her eyes widened in surprise. She was dressed much the way she'd been on Friday night, in black stretch pants and a loose-fitting top. This one was a slightly deeper shade of blue than her eyes and it had better coverage.

"Hi," she said. "I thought you might be Betsy."

"No, I'm me." Duh. That must have sounded brilliant.

"Well, come on in, you." She opened the door a little wider and tossed her hair over one shoulder.

That reminded him of how easily those soft blond strands had become tangled in his watch strap. He hadn't realized until she invited him in that he'd been hoping she would. To his surprise, though, the small space looked like a head-on collision between a craft store and a flea market.

"I just made a pot of coffee," she said. "Decaf. Would you like some?"

Coffee and a little conversation would beat going downstairs and spending the rest of the evening lost in his own thoughts. "Sounds good. Thanks."

"Grab a spot in the living room. I'll bring it in."

The "living room" was separated from the kitchen by the sofa. The cat was curled up and asleep on the only chair, so Mitch pushed aside a blanket and sat at one end of the sofa. The coffee table was strewn with colored construction paper, scissors, markers and glue. There were several things under the table, including a pair of pink feathery shoes. If there was ever a pair of shoes not meant to be worn outside a bedroom, this was it.

"Cream and sugar?" she asked.

"Black is good."

"Sorry about the mess." She handed him a mug and shoved most of the paper into a pile so she could set her own on the coffee table. "I'm working on a couple of school projects and lesson plans." She sat at the other end of the sofa with her back against the arm, pulled her feet up and wrapped her arms around her knees.

He wanted to ask about the shoes, and he tried not to look at her feet, he really did, but the nails had been painted with grape-colored polish and her delicately formed toes had his fingers itching to touch them. She wriggled them a little and he dragged his gaze away. When he looked up, he realized she'd been watching him.

"My friend Nicola called yesterday to tell me you're in the wedding party."

Did she think that was why he was here? "Yeah. I was kind of surprised, but I don't mind pinch-hitting. Jonathan's a nice guy."

"I didn't ask them to ask you, I swear. I didn't know anything about it till just now."

He believed her. Now for the million-dollar question. "Are you going with someone?" As soon as he asked, he wished he hadn't. That was not why he was here. And what if she said yes?

"Are you asking if I have a date?"

He swallowed hard. "I guess I am."

Her smile took the edge off his nerves. "No, I don't. What about you?"

Him? A date? He shook his head.

"We could go together. It doesn't have to be a date unless you want it to be."

"Sure." Not much of an answer, but he couldn't bring himself to say yes, though he *did* want it to be.

"More coffee?"

He hadn't realized his cup was empty. "Sure."

She got up, refilled it and curled up on the sofa again. "There was a report about a fire on the news. Was that your station?"

"It was."

"I thought so. Was everyone okay? Nicola called and I missed the end of the story."

"As far as I know, everyone's fine. The house was gutted, though. I sure hope they had insurance because I'd say they lost pretty much everything."

She hugged her knees a little tighter. "So sad. It was great that the dog was rescued, though. They showed that on the news."

Of course they did. They probably spent more time talking about the dog than the woman who saved the lives of her two children. "We always get extra media coverage when a pet is rescued. Reporters love that sort of thing."

Rory laughed. "It's heroic. Everyone expects you to rescue people, but when someone goes the extra mile for an animal, that really tugs at the heartstrings."

She was probably right. "Actually, the reason I came up here...Miranda told me about the jacket."

Something that resembled guilt flickered across her face, and then just as quickly she was smiling. Had he misinterpreted what he saw? "I'm sorry. I should have asked you first but she didn't have her jacket when we went to pick up supplies for Nicola's bridal shower and I happened to have that one with me, so I gave it to her."

"No problem." He took out his wallet. "I want to pay you for it, though. How much was it?"

She shook her head strenuously. "Don't worry about it. Like I said, I already had it."

"She said it was a gift for someone. Don't you have to buy another one?"

The guilty look was back, no mistake about it. "I can't take any money for it."

"Why not?"

She looked up at him, very serious, and for a few seconds—quite a few—she didn't say anything. "It wasn't a gift," she said finally. "Well, it was, but not for someone else. I bought it for Miranda."

It took him a moment to respond. "Um…why?"

She let out a long sigh. "Her blue jacket is too small. While I was shopping with a friend last Saturday, I saw the yellow one and bought it. After I brought it home I realized it wasn't my place to interfere and I was going to take it back, but she didn't have a jacket when we were out yesterday and it was cold so…" She gave an expansive shrug. "I'm sorry."

Now it was his turn to feel guilty. He admired her honesty, and she was right about the old jacket being too small. "Don't apologize. She's growing like a weed and she does need new clothes. Shopping isn't really my thing." Even as he said it, it sounded lame.

"I'm sure Betsy would help if you asked."

"She would, but she has her own life and she already does so much for us that I hate to ask." He drained his mug and set it on the table. "Thanks for the coffee," he said. "I think I should go." He took another look at the pink shoes and considered changing his mind. She was easy to talk to, she genuinely seemed to care about Miranda and aside from that, who was he kidding? She was gorgeous, and he wanted to kiss her now just as much as he had last Friday.

They both stood and she walked with him to the door.

"Thanks for coming up." She stepped closer and lightly ran her hand along his upper arm.

He brushed her hair back off her shoulders. "I'm still not sure this is a good idea."

"Neither am I, but at least your mother won't walk in on us up here."

Good point, and yet neither of them moved. He wanted to move, desperately wanted to kiss her, but he didn't and he didn't know why. Instead he backed away, closed the door and was halfway down the stairs before he realized he hadn't paid for the jacket. He wasn't going back, no matter how much he wanted to, and God knew he wanted to.

RORY RESTED HER FOREHEAD against the door and listened to the sound of footsteps fading down the stairs.

What on earth are you doing? Making a date to go to a wedding with a family man who hasn't been on the market in...what? A decade?

Her father's words echoed in her mind. *He's a good man, Rory. A good father.*

There was no question about that, but she wasn't looking for a man, not even a good one. Or was she? After almost being kissed by him, she wasn't so sure.

And then there were Jess's bull's-eye observations and sage advice. *Your dad's right. You've got it bad.*

No, she didn't.

Are you sure that being a stand-in mom is the best way to go about this?

Jess was crazy. Rory wasn't a stand-in anything, and she wasn't using Miranda to get to Mitch. She enjoyed spending time with Miranda and felt sorry for the little girl who'd lost her mother. She felt sorry for Mitch, too, but she wasn't a stand-in.

She *was* letting her emotions get the best of her, though.

She sat on the sofa and took a sip of her coffee. Ugh. It was cold. She grabbed Mitch's mug and carried both to the kitchen counter. After she rinsed hers and set it in the sink, she curled her fingers around his, remembering how he'd held it, and how she had admired the shape and strength of his hands.

Had he gone out with another woman since his wife's accident?

Instinct told her the answer was no, and yet he had readily agreed to go the wedding with her. Did that mean he was interested? Without a doubt, she knew the answer to that question was yes.

If you play with fire, you'll eventually get burned.

She had no idea who had said that, but it was probably the best advice so far.

"I WANT TO PUSH THE garage-door button," Miranda said the next morning when they backed out onto the street.

Mitch stopped, unclipped the remote from the visor and passed it back to her. He took a quick look up the street while she watched the door roll shut, and there was Rory kneeling on the sidewalk.

What was that in front of her? A toolbox?

She took out a wrench, studied it and put it back, and took out another. Car trouble?

He backed out onto the street and pulled into a parking space. "It looks like Ro...Miss Sunshine is having trouble with her van. Can you sit tight for a few minutes, princess? I'll see if she needs some help."

"'Kay."

He got out and walked up the sidewalk.

The van's side doors were open and Rory was standing behind the vehicle, wrench in hand, talking to someone. "What is your *problem?* I have to get downtown!"

Correction. She was talking to the van.

"Is everything okay?"

She looked relieved to see him. "No. Do you know anything about engines?"

Not much. "What's the problem?"

She shrugged. "It won't start."

"Is there gas in the tank?"

"I filled it the other day." She glanced over his shoulder

and then back at him, looking puzzled. "Why is your garage door going up and down?"

He turned around and sure enough, the door was open and now it was closing, again. "Miranda's waiting in the car for me. She must be playing with the remote."

Rory laughed. "That's funny. Are you on your way out?"

"We are. Shopping for clothes. She's pretty much out-grown everything." After Rory had admitted to giving Miranda the jacket because her old one didn't fit, he'd known he couldn't put this off any longer.

She nodded her approval. "You should go then. I'll figure something out."

"Where do you have to go?" he asked.

"Downtown. I have another dress-fitting at the bridal salon and I have to pick up a few things for Nic's shower tomorrow afternoon. Where are you going shopping?"

It was his turn to shrug. "Not sure. We can give you a lift downtown and then figure it out from there."

"Would you? That would be great. And Macy's always has great sales."

"Then Macy's it is." He took the wrench from her and put it in the toolbox. "Where would you like me to put this?"

"In the back is fine. I'll grab my purse and lock up."

He set the toolbox on the floor in the back of the van and wished he wasn't so intrigued by the tiny living space—especially the bed—and closed the doors. After she locked them, they walked to his SUV together. The garage door opened again, and this time they both laughed.

"I don't suppose..." He hesitated.

"What?"

"I thought maybe, that is, would you like to go shopping with us? I mean, I know you're busy, but—"

She stopped walking and reached for his arm. "If you

don't mind waiting at the bridal salon—I have to make sure my dress fits—I'd love to. It'll be fun."

THE IMPROMPTU SHOPPING trip with Mitch and Miranda had been even more fun than Rory had expected. Miranda had enjoyed being the center of attention and, like a little princess-in-training, loved trying on new things and modeling them for her father. She was now outfitted with two new pairs of jeans for school, an armload of cozy winter T-shirts and sweaters, socks, underwear and the most adorable pair of pale yellow polka-dot flannelette pajamas.

Rory had also quietly convinced Mitch to splurge on a new dress—the "twirly" kind—that Miranda could wear to Nic and Jonathan's wedding ceremony. Although she wasn't on the guest list, Betsy could take her to the church. Knowing how excited she would get, Mitch had asked that it be a surprise, so he simply told her the new dress was for special occasions.

Now they were seated in a booth at a fifties-themed diner, Mitch on one side next to a pile of shopping bags, and Rory and Miranda seated on the other.

The server's purple-streaked hair, eyebrow ring and the dragon tattoo on her shoulder were an amusing contrast to the James Dean posters and the retro chrome-and-Arborite decor.

At least Rory was amused. Mitch not so much.

Miranda dumped crayons out of a small cup and studied the farm scene on her paper place mat. "I already know what I'm having. The kid's cheeseburger." She picked up the red crayon and started on the barn. "And fries." She sounded definite, but looked hopefully at her father. "I can have fries, right?"

He nodded.

The waitress looked at Rory.

"I'll have a BLT on toasted multigrain."

"Soup, salad or fries with that?"

Rory winked at Miranda. "I'll have fries, too. And coffee, please."

"And you, sir?"

"I'll have the cheeseburger. And fries," he added quickly, before she launched into the choices again. "And coffee."

She jotted his order on her notepad and turned to Rory again as she gathered up the menus. "What would your daughter like to drink?"

It was the third time that morning that someone had mistaken her for Miranda's mother, and for the third time she offered a correction. It was an honest enough mistake, given they both had blond hair and blue eyes, but every time it happened, Mitch's expression became more difficult to decipher. If he hadn't been with them, she'd have been tempted not to make the correction, but she didn't dare let anyone, even a stranger, assume she was his wife.

"I'm just a friend, not her mother."

The server couldn't have been less interested.

Rory lightly touched Miranda's arm to get her attention. "What would you like to drink?"

Miranda stopped coloring. "A chocolate milkshake."

Mitch shook his head. "How about a glass of milk?"

"Chocolate milk?" she asked, ever hopeful.

He gently shook his head again, the negative answer tempered by an affectionate smile.

The waitress made a note of the milk and walked away.

Miranda grinned at Rory. "It's pretty funny that everybody thinks you're my mom."

"I think it's because our hair is the same color."

Miranda ran a hand over Rory's hair. "I wish mine was long like yours."

Rory resisted the urge to ask how Miranda's mother had worn hers. "Your hair suits you perfectly."

Miranda leaned close and touched the side of her head to Rory's. "What do you think, Dad? Do we have the same hair?"

Mitch cleared his throat and then took a gulp of his ice water.

Rory held her breath. She couldn't begin to guess what he was thinking, but she hoped he'd say yes.

"It looks the same to me."

She exhaled slowly. His answer didn't come out quite the way she'd hoped it would, but his eyes were telling a different story. *So, Mitch Donovan. Is there anything else about me that reminds you of your wife?* She hoped not. But if there was, would that be a bad thing? Yes. She meant what she'd said to Jess—she didn't want to be anybody's stand-in.

The server appeared with two cups of coffee and a glass of milk. Miranda picked up her drinking straw and peeled off the paper wrapper. Then she handed a green crayon to Rory. "You can color the tree if you want."

"Okay." Rory took the crayon and started filling in the outline. "What kind of tree do you think this is?"

"I don't know. Maybe an apple tree?"

"Would you like me to put some apples in it?"

"'Kay. Here's the red crayon."

She drew a couple of apples and finished coloring the rest of the tree.

"My mom used to color with me."

Rory set the crayon on the table. Again, Mitch's reaction was indecipherable.

"Have you been to this restaurant before?" Rory asked.

"Yup. My mom liked it here."

Rory watched for Mitch's reaction but he was looking at something out the window as though he hadn't heard.

When their meals arrived, Rory quickly helped Miranda clear away the crayons. "One kid's cheeseburger," the server said.

"Yum. I *love* French fries." Miranda bit into one and spat it onto her plate. "Hot!"

Her father gave her a stern look, but Rory handed her a glass of water. "Drink this, quick. It'll stop the burning."

The server set down Mitch's burger and Rory's sandwich. "Can I get you anything else?"

Rory smiled up at her. "No, thanks."

"Miranda, remember your manners. You don't start eating till everyone has their meal, remember?"

"I was just so excited to try a fry 'cause I haven't had them for ages."

"Ketchup?" Mitch held up the bottle.

"Yup." She reached for it. "I can put it on myself."

She watched Mitch reluctantly hand the red plastic bottle to his daughter.

Miranda squirted a generous blob onto the pile of fries on her plate and a little dribble on the table.

"Good job," Rory said. She swiped the ketchup off the table with a paper napkin as she nodded at Mitch across the table, hoping he understood that Miranda needed to do things for herself, even if meant sometimes making a mess.

Miranda passed the bottle to Rory. "Do you like ketchup?

"You bet I do. Thanks." She squirted some beside her French fries, set the bottle on the table and slowly slid it across to Mitch.

"Have you ever gone on a cable car?" Miranda asked.

She had, once, and the downhill trip to Fisherman's

Wharf had kind of freaked her out. "I have, but the steep part was pretty scary."

"Not for me. Someday me and my dad are going on one again. If you come with us, maybe you won't be scared."

Having two hands to hold could be fun and it just might help. Mitch's response was less than favorable, though. Either he didn't want to ride on a cable car at all, or he didn't want to ride on one with her.

"We'll see," she said to Miranda. "But that might be something you and your dad should do on your own."

What are you doing? she asked herself for the umpteenth time. Mitch might not be looking for a replacement wife, but there were times when it seemed as though his daughter was looking for a replacement mother. And Rory had to admit that all morning she had been entertaining the idea as though it was a real possibility. It wasn't. She could not, would not be a stand-in for Miranda's mother.

Chapter Eleven

Rory felt inexplicably jittery on the day of Nicola's wedding, and she didn't know why. Maybe it was the weather. She gazed up through her skylight, grateful that the rain that had threatened all day was still holding off. Nic had already called three times that morning, and each time Rory had been able to calm her down and assure her that everything would be perfect, no matter what the weather was like. After tonight, though, she'd have two weeks of peace and quiet. Nic would be on her honeymoon but her BlackBerry, at Jonathan's insistence, was staying in San Francisco.

And Rory never had to be a maid of honor again.

Everything had gone smoothly, though, including the bridal shower. The guests had raved about the food, the decorations and the stunning view of the bay. Even the table centerpieces had been perfect, and Rory was beyond grateful to Nic's mom for doing most of the work. Still, she would be happy to simply be a bridesmaid if Jess ever tied the knot, or if Paige got married again.

Rory stripped off her dressing gown and avoided looking at herself in the full-length mirror. She'd bought the shoes and lingerie with Mitch in mind, and that now felt like a mistake. When she'd had lunch with him and Miranda—which had been only two weeks ago but felt more like a lifetime—he hadn't been at all happy that everyone mistook her for Miranda's mother.

Well, neither had she. She couldn't replace his wife and she wasn't interested in trying, so the best thing to do was put a little distance between them. In spite of living in such close quarters, avoiding him had been surprisingly easy. He was a creature of habit, and it had been easy to figure out how to avoid running into him. Of course that had meant paying close attention to when he came and went, but she'd had to do it.

She removed the dress from the hanger and stepped into it, taking care not to hook the heel of her shoes in the netting under the full skirt. She managed to zip it up and, after a few minor contortions, even managed the hook-and-eye closing at the top. She had run into Mitch the other day— she was pretty sure it was deliberate on his part—and he had asked what time she had to leave for the wedding. Since they had to spend the day together anyway—*although it's not a date,* she reminded herself—they might as well drive together. And that meant they had to leave in…she glanced at the clock radio next to her bed…ten minutes.

She fluffed her hair and applied another layer of lipstick. The dress swished against Buick's chair as she made her way across the room, and he gave her a one-eyed glare.

"You get an early dinner today," she said, and made her way into the kitchen. She was hungry, too, but didn't think she could eat anything if she tried. "I'm just nervous about the wedding," she said to Buick. It was the responsibility of being a maid of honor that was making her stomach do cartwheels, not the prospect of spending the day with Mitch.

MITCH FELT LIKE A teenager on a first date. Since the shopping trip and lunch with Miranda two weeks ago, he and

Rory had settled into a comfortable pattern of greeting each other as they came and went from the house, or when he took Miranda to school and picked her up, but there'd been no more close encounters. Something had changed that day in the restaurant, but he hadn't been able to figure out why. Whatever it was, Rory seemed a little inaccessible.

Now as he stood in the foyer and looked up the stairs, he wasn't sure if he should go up there, but it seemed no amount of wishing would make Rory appear. She needed to be at the bride's home an hour before the wedding, which meant they had to leave soon or they'd never make it. He'd better go up and see if she was ready. Her door was open but he knocked anyway.

"Come in. I just need to feed Buick and then we can go."

He stepped inside. "No problem." The cat was curled up in the same chair, asleep, in pretty much the same position as the last time he was here.

Rory was at the kitchen counter. Some of her hair had been swept back from her face, and all of it cascaded down her back in big, soft, golden waves. His fingers flexed in anticipation. There'd be dancing at the reception, so he'd have a perfectly legitimate reason to touch her.

Schloop. She popped the lid off the can and the cat leaped to attention. He jumped off the chair and had Rory laughing as he tried to rub himself against the full skirt of her dress. One foot in a strappy sparkly high-heeled shoe appeared from beneath the dress and gently nudged him away. It was the kind of shoe that was not meant to be hidden.

"Cut it out," she said. "I don't want cat hair all over my dress."

She glanced over her shoulder and grinned at Mitch. "I should have fed him *before* I got ready."

The cat continued to circle the dress, living up to his name by filling the small space with the sound of his purring while she spooned his food into a dish. The cat lost interest in her the instant she set his dish on the floor. She picked up her keys and a tote bag that was hanging from the back of a kitchen chair. "All set."

He had seen the dress the day she'd gone shopping with him and Miranda, but he hadn't seen her in it. She looked as though she'd stepped off the page of a magazine, and he still couldn't quite believe she had walked into his life.

He worked up the courage to ask the question that had been on his mind for two weeks. "Is everything okay?"

"I don't know what you mean." She sounded cautious, though, and he got the sense that maybe she did.

"Since lunch that day, you've been, I don't know, distant."

At first she didn't say anything. Instead she opened the bag and appeared to be checking that she had everything she needed. "I'm sorry," she said finally. "I realized you were uncomfortable when everyone kept mistaking me for Miranda's mother, and then she kept talking to me about her mom…" She closed the bag again. "I guess I should have said something."

Like what? That you don't want a family? She had a way with kids and she'd be a wonderful mother, in spite of her declaration of independence—a declaration that seemed oddly out of character now that he was getting to know her. It had contradicted what appeared to be a strong maternal instinct, one so strong that even Miranda had picked up on it.

He wasn't ready to rush into a committed relationship, either, but he'd been hoping… "We hardly know each other, but Miranda thinks the world of you, and I…ah…" *Say it.* "I kind of enjoyed having coffee together." And the kiss.

Rory's face softened into a smile. "Me, too." She extended a hand. "Friends?"

He held it without shaking it. "Friends." The afternoon and evening ahead of them suddenly held a lot more promise.

His mother met them at the front door and, somewhat to his surprise, she was wearing a brown-and-yellow flowered broomstick skirt and a deep-gold-colored gypsy-style top reminiscent of her youth. Her hair, in its usual single braid, had been twisted around her head. If she had considered tucking flowers into it, and most likely she had, he was relieved she had resisted.

Rory hugged her. "Betsy, you look gorgeous! We should put some flowers in your hair."

"Pretty sure we don't have time," Mitch said.

"You're right," Rory said. "I don't want to keep Nicola waiting."

"That's quite a dress," Betsy said. "Isn't it a tradition for the bride and her bridesmaids to get ready for the wedding together?"

"We did when my other friends got married, but Nicola tends to stress about stuff like that, so I suggested we get ready on our own and meet before the wedding. We'll still have plenty of time to take photos and make last-minute adjustments before we take the limo to the church."

Miranda skipped across the living room, the skirt of her new blue dress swishing from side to side. He had waited till this morning to tell her she could go to the church, and she'd been bubbling with excitement ever since. "Miss Sunshine, your dress is beautiful."

Rory gave her a mock curtsy. "Thank you. You look pretty beautiful yourself."

Miranda pointed to the blue headband that held her curls off her face. "Grams bought this to go with my dress."

"It matches perfectly."

"And we match, too. We're both wearing blue."

He watched to see if Rory would take exception to the look-alike reference. If she did, she didn't let on.

"We should go," Mitch said, holding the front door open. He had parked on the street so Rory wouldn't have to go down the basement stairs in her dress.

"I was wondering if I could borrow your van," Betsy asked. "I thought I'd take Miranda out for dinner after the ceremony."

"Of course." Rory offered her keys.

"Va-nna White, Va-nna White." Miranda emphasized each syllable by hopping three times on one foot, then three times on the other.

The idea of his daughter being a passenger in that motorized scrap yard, especially with his mother at the wheel, had his gut churning. "Does your van have a stick shift?" he asked, already knowing the answer.

"It does. Is that a problem?"

"Oh…" Betsy said. "It's been a while since I've driven one."

"Then you should take my car," Mitch offered. "Rory and I can take the van." His mother would have an easier time with an automatic, and Miranda would be a lot safer.

"Good idea." Rory handed her keys to him instead. "Would you mind driving? I don't think there's room for me *and* the dress in the driver's seat."

He smiled at her as he pocketed the keys. "Sure."

On the front porch, Miranda stood on one foot and spun herself around. "Look at my dress," she called to them. "It's all floaty."

He opened the passenger door and held Rory's bag so she could get in—not an easy feat in that dress and those shoes. He offered her a hand and she finally settled into the passenger seat. "Mine's a little too floaty," she muttered, stuffing her dress around her knees and covering her feet. The shoes were such a distraction that he still hadn't noticed the color of her polish.

MITCH'S DAUGHTER WAVED at him as he and the other groomsmen took their places at the front of the church. He nodded and smiled at her, feeling quite certain that the bride would disapprove of a waving usher. Without a doubt, Rory's friend Nicola was one of the most intense people he'd ever met, and certainly not the type of woman he would have pictured easygoing Jonathan spending the rest of his life with. But true to character, Jonathan was looking relaxed and supremely confident. Mitch tried to remember the way he'd felt on his own wedding day, but the memories escaped him.

The organist was playing something suitably matrimonial. The melody was familiar, although Mitch couldn't place it.

On the one hand, he felt like a complete fraud for being here at all. On the other, he'd been looking forward to spending the afternoon and evening with Rory. He would never have asked her out on a real date. Given their living situation and that she was Miranda's teacher, dating her didn't seem like the appropriate thing to do. His mother and his daughter didn't seem to have a problem with it, and he was starting to believe that Laura probably wouldn't, either. He did, however, and although he wasn't sure why, he wasn't ready to examine his feelings about this. For now, having her for a friend was all he needed.

From where he stood, he could see Miranda and his mother sitting midway down the church. His daughter sat still, her usual well-behaved self, but her bobbing blond curls gave away her excitement. The bride had thoughtfully invited her to the ceremony, but he was relieved she wouldn't be at the reception. Not that he planned to do anything inappropriate, but Miranda had already developed the romantic notion that he needed a wife, and that Rory would make a great mom. And she was right—someday Rory would be good as both.

A sudden change in the tempo of the organ music coincided with the opening of the double doors at the back of the church. The first bridesmaid appeared. She was a generously proportioned brunette with dark-framed glasses, an uncertain smile and incredibly gentle brown eyes. As she took her place near the altar, the next bridesmaid began the trek. This one had flashing dark eyes and a smile that lit up the church. She was the pregnant one Rory had mentioned. Very pregnant, and it obviously suited her. She bounced into position next to the timid-looking woman and squeezed her hand.

The third bridesmaid was a tall, reedy redhead with a don't-mess-with-me expression. Mitch couldn't help smiling as she strode gracelessly toward the others. The only thing missing was her lawn mower. He'd put money on this one being the bartender.

And then Rory appeared, walking down the aisle with a smile that heated his blood and blurred his senses like a shot of whiskey. And she wasn't even smiling at him.

God, she was beautiful.

She had made it clear that she hated the dress, but the way it emphasized her stunning blond hair and the perfect shape of her breasts, well, he kind of liked it.

He glanced quickly at his mother. For a few seconds he'd forgotten she was here. Had she noticed his assessment of her new tenant?

Yes, she had.

She was giving him that self-satisfied look of hers, the

one that said she knew exactly what he'd been thinking as he watched Rory glide down the aisle. He knew exactly what his mother was thinking right now. And somewhat to his surprise, he didn't care. He gave her a hint of a nod that he hoped no one else would notice. As the bride took her place next to the groom, Mitch realized he hadn't seen her come into the church. All his attention had been on Rory and what had felt like her walking into his life.

When the ceremony was over, Mitch couldn't remember any more about it than he could about his own wedding, but not for the same reason. While the minister had welcomed everyone, Mitch had glanced at Rory and she'd glanced at him and they'd both quickly looked away. Each time it happened, their gazes held a little longer. The tension caused by their mutual awareness of each other eased, gradually, and as it did, the connection between them seemed to grow stronger. In spite of the distance between them, it felt like physical contact.

Thinking back on the few occasions when there *had* been physical contact, it had been nothing short of mind-boggling. His mother or his daughter had always been around, though, and that had prevented anything from coming of it. Tonight, he'd have plenty of opportunities to be close to Rory, and there'd be no family around to catch them. The prospect of escorting her onto the dance floor, touching the soft-looking skin on her shoulders and losing his fingers in her hair was exhilarating and terrifying. He wished he could fast-forward to that moment.

The audience stood and applauded as the minister presented the newlyweds, the organ music swelled and the bride and groom led the procession up the aisle.

All right, he thought. *Let's get this party started.*

"Dance with me?"

Finally. Rory let Mitch help her to her feet. "I thought you'd never ask."

"I was beginning to wonder if I'd ever get a chance."

He wasn't the only one. After the ceremony there had been a two-hour session with the photographer, then the receiving line that had taken forever, followed by cocktails, dinner and speeches.

Throughout all of it, Rory had been paired with Jonathan's brother, the best man, and Mitch was with Jess. Since they had arrived at the church, they'd only exchanged a few words. Now, finally, they had a few moments together.

She followed him onto the dance floor, placed one hand in his and all but melted into his arms.

"Has Jess been keeping you amused?"

Mitch grinned. "She's very entertaining."

Not *too* entertaining, Rory hoped. Every time she'd looked at them, they'd been talking and laughing like old friends. She'd never seen him look so relaxed and, well, happy. Meanwhile, she and the best man—no doubt a very smart guy but a computer geek to the core—had quickly discovered they had nothing in common but the bride and groom.

"She's the only bartender with a brown belt in karate I've ever met, and she's a big fan of yours."

"Really?" Rory asked cautiously. "What did she say?"

"You're great with kids. You'll make a wonderful mother someday. If I didn't know better, I might have thought she was trying to set us up."

"She didn't!" But Rory knew she had, and now she wasn't so much worried that Jess and Mitch had hit it off as she was that Jess's endorsement was exactly what Mitch thought it might be, and she had a hunch that Jess wasn't working alone. Now that things were going well, she didn't need their meddling. "She was just getting back at me for making her go shopping."

Her response seemed to disappoint him. "She doesn't like to shop?"

"She hates it. Especially for shoes and lingerie."

"Ah, the shoes. She did a lot of complaining about those. Didn't mention the lingerie, though…" He glanced across the banquet room to where Jess was standing, as though looking at her with renewed interest.

Rory was pretty sure he was teasing her. "She's very attractive, don't you think?"

"Beautiful," he said, but his gaze had returned to her. "Especially the hair." The hand on her back moved higher and she could tell that her own hair was now threaded through his fingers.

"I was hoping you preferred blondes."

He held her a little closer, and she let him. "And if I did?"

"It would make you a gentleman."

"Then blondes it is."

Banter didn't come naturally to Mitch, but he was more relaxed than she'd ever seen him. And it just so happened that a relaxed Mitch was an excellent dancer and…oh. He moved his hand even higher and a warm fingertip stroked her skin just above the top of her dress.

She opened her mouth to respond to *Then blondes it is,* but there were no words. Oh, well. Talking was highly overrated. Besides, who needed words when body language said it all?

She rested her cheek against his shoulder and closed her eyes. He was different from any man she'd ever met, and that was exciting and scary and unsettling all at the same time. She was her own person and she didn't need a man to make her feel complete—she could do that for herself. But why was it different with Mitch? With him and Miranda, she felt like more of a person than she could be on her own. Not that she'd ever felt incomplete, but they made her want to be part of a greater whole—part of the traditional family she'd never had. One that lived and played...and stayed together.

The band's female vocalist was singing a sultry, ultra-sexy rendition of "Baby, I Need Your Loving." Mitch's hands and those lyrics were making her think about how good it would feel to be with a man again. Especially this one. She didn't know exactly where he stood on that, but if she took things slow, gave him time to get used to the idea...

The music stopped and the dancers applauded. Rory opened her eyes and blinked, not even close to being ready for the dance to end. A few couples left the dance floor, others waited for the next song. She and Mitch exchanged frustrated glances when the band launched into an up-tempo modern-sounding number she couldn't put a name to.

"Want to get some fresh air?" he asked.

"Yes."

They slipped through a side door that led to a terrace. Several clusters of people had gathered there, some seated at small, cloth-covered tables, others standing in small groups. He took her hand, she laced her fingers between his and they walked toward the dimly lit grounds.

For a few minutes they kept up the pretense of going for a stroll through the immaculately groomed gardens of the country club. Not an ideal place for making out, but Rory didn't much care. She doubted Mitch did, either. When he led her off the path beneath the overhanging boughs of a tree and took her into his arms, she went eagerly, lifted her face up to his and waited. This time she'd let him kiss her first.

But he didn't. "You must be cold," he said instead.

"A little." The air was cool on her bare arms and shoulders, but she could think of any number of ways to warm them up.

He shrugged off his jacket and held it out for her. She slipped it on, liking the feel of his body heat on her skin and the hint of musky male scent that might be cologne or aftershave, or maybe just him. Either way, it suited him and it totally worked for her.

"Now you'll be cold."

"No, I won't." He braced himself against the tree and put his arms around her, under the jacket, and then kissed her. His mouth was firm but gentle, like the rest of him, and then he drew her in for some full body contact and things got a little more intense and a lot more firm.

"I've wanted to do this ever since I met you," he said.

"Me, too." The heels of her shoes sank into the lawn, so she tried to balance on her toes.

His mouth reconnected with hers, this time with a little tongue that sent sparks all the way down to those toes, and then the tantalizing way his fingers were exploring the top edge of her dress, as though looking for a way in, sent another round. She kissed him and he kissed her back and things were heating up nicely in all the nicest places, and then her shoes started to sink into the grass again. Damn.

"What's wrong?" he asked.

"It's too hard to stand on the grass in these shoes."

"Maybe we should go back inside."

"Is that what you want?" she asked.

"No."

That made two of them. "My van is in the parking lot. You have the keys, don't you?"

"Yes." His voice sounded deep and husky.

So much for taking this slowly.

MITCH FUMBLED WITH THE KEYS.

"Let me do it," Rory said. "Vanna's locks are temperamental."

He let her take the keys. In a flash, she swung the side doors open.

She scrunched the voluminous dress in her hands and tried to climb in. All day he had been getting glimpses of sparkly, barely-there shoes and mother-of-pearl toes, but the damn shoes were no better at climbing than they were at standing on the lawn. He grasped her slender waist and helped her inside, then climbed in behind her. Their combined weight set the van rocking.

Rory giggled as she tumbled onto the bed, and she was still giggling when she pulled him down on top of her. This was crazy. The van was still rocking, and he was pretty sure the vehicle hadn't been constructed with this kind of thing in mind.

He'd been imagining this for days. Well, not exactly *this*. In his fantasy, the bed wasn't on wheels and Rory wasn't giggling, but his guilt was gone. Like it was now. And she was ready and willing, like he was. Now.

She smelled of oranges and roses and sunshine—he liked that—and when he kissed her, she tasted even sweeter. It seemed forever since he'd felt this alive and this ready to be guided by physical needs. Rory's warm and inviting body, sprawled beneath his, was rapidly escalating those needs to must-haves.

He couldn't gain access to the top of her dress so he explored the contour of her breasts from the outside. Imagining them naked in his palm didn't take much. Beneath him, her hips moved in the unmistakable rhythm he had dreamed of.

"Lift up for a second," she said.

Separating himself from her was next to impossible, but he did what she asked. She hitched her dress up around her waist. Now the only thing separating them were his clothes and whatever she had on under the dress. There was only one way to find out what that was.

He traced a hasty route up the inside of one warm, accommodating thigh till the tips of his fingers met the warm, silky smoothness of her panties.

"Take them off," she whispered, sending a gush of warm air into one ear that zinged all the way down his spine.

So soon?

"Mitch?"

Who was he to question a woman who obviously knew what she wanted? He hooked a finger under a silk strap and slid the flimsy garment over her hips and down her legs. While he fumbled one side over the heel of those delectable shoes, she went to work on his fly. Her fingers glided over his erection as the zipper rasped open.

She tried to push his pants down over his hips. "Help me out here."

Bossy little thing. Well, she wouldn't get an argument from him—turned out he liked a woman who knew what she wanted. While he finished what she had started, she twisted sideways and opened a small compartment above the bed.

"Here." She shoved a box into his hands.

Condoms. Of course. Good idea. He definitely didn't want to be involved in a backseat conception. Besides, Volkswagen would be a hell of a name for a cat.

The box was still sealed, which he found vaguely reassuring, but in the dim light that filtered through the

curtains, he couldn't see how to open it. He pried at what
he thought was the flap.

Come on.

To make matters worse, his hands were shaking.
Badly.

The cardboard finally gave way. The strip of plastic-
wrapped condoms leaped out of the carton and unfurled
itself on Rory's chest like some kind of perverted jack-in-
the-box.

She giggled again, tore one packet off the strip and
handed it to him, and tossed the rest aside. Then those
naughty little fingers explored his midsection while he
struggled to tear open the plastic.

He should tell her to stop, or at least slow down. More
than a year of celibacy was about to come to an end, but
he didn't want it to end *this* way.

"Let me have it," she said.

"What?" She couldn't be serious.

"The condom. Give it to me." He could tell she was
smiling at his misunderstanding.

The plastic gave her no trouble, but he was glad she
handed the unwrapped condom back to him. This part he
could manage on his own. What he couldn't handle was
much more of her handling.

And then waiting and wanting were over. Entering her
was like crossing the threshold to a perfect paradise, and
being inside her felt mind-numbingly good. The months
of abstinence had done wonders for his sex drive, but they
were having the opposite effect on his self-control.

He wanted this to be just as good for her. No, better.

Maybe if he slowed down a little.

He withdrew almost completely, then slowly entered
her again. It seemed like a good plan, and it should have
worked.

It didn't.

His orgasm was sudden and not particularly satisfying.

Damn it. Damn it, damn it, damn it.

He rested his forehead against hers. "Sorry."

She moved insistently beneath him. "Can you still…you know?"

He couldn't bring himself to say it out loud so he just shook his head. His traitorous libido was already retreating. He lifted himself off her, mentally scrambling to think of some way to get them both out of this clumsy entanglement with some shred of dignity. There wasn't one.

Rory had other ideas. She put her hands on his shoulders and pushed downward, a silent communication that left no doubt about what she wanted.

He complied.

Her climax was almost as spontaneous as his had been, but judging by her prolonged movements and the soft, throaty sounds she made, it was infinitely more satisfying. Her hands were still in his hair when she finally stopped moving, and then she withdrew them, propped herself on her elbows and smiled down at him. "*That* was amazing."

"I'm glad." He should say something else, but what? *This has never happened before.* Like she'd care. *It's been a while.* He was pretty sure she'd already figured that out. Thanks to his ill-timed orgasm there was no retrieving his dignity, and now they had to go back inside with her friends and act like none of this had happened.

Maybe when they got home…

Hell, who was he kidding? More than anything he wanted to make love to her properly, in a proper bed, but there was no way he'd risk a repeat of this performance again tonight.

HAND IN HAND, Rory and Mitch quickly covered the distance between the parking lot and the reception hall. In the dark she couldn't get a read on what he was thinking, which made his brooding silence that much harder to take. She wanted to say something but had no idea what that should be.

He dropped her hand as they approached the terrace. Disappointed, she grabbed his arm and stopped walking. He stopped, too, and finally looked at her. Although the outdoor lighting was still too dim to get a good look at his face, she knew he wasn't happy about their tryst in the van.

"Why did you let go of my hand?" she asked.

"I assumed you wouldn't want your friends to see us."

She slipped her arms around his waist and briefly rested her head against his chest. "I don't care who sees us." It was true. She didn't.

"Are you sure?"

"They've already figured out something's going on, so yeah, I'm fine with it. What about you?" She lifted her head and waited.

He didn't answer right away, and that scared her.

"About what happened back there—" He tipped his head in the direction of the parking lot. "I'm sorry."

If she had learned anything from her parents' many mistakes, it was not to let misunderstandings fester into a major falling-out. "Are you sorry it happened, or sorry it happened so fast?"

Again, no response, and if she had to guess, she'd say he was blushing. Ah, yes. Nothing quite so fragile as the male ego.

"In case you didn't notice, I was in a bit of a hurry myself. Next time will be better." To demonstrate how much better, she kissed him—a hungry, openmouthed kiss with lots of tongue—and slid one hand along the fly of his pants. Her touch made him suck in a sharp breath, and the rest of him responded accordingly.

She tipped her head back and smiled at him, leaving her hand where it was. "Better for both of us," she whispered. He pressed himself into her hand and kissed her back, even hungrier.

Oh, yeah, she thought. *Next time will blow your mind.*

MITCH GAZED UP THROUGH Rory's skylight and watched the night sky begin to lighten while she slept, her invitingly warm body curled against his. It had been quite a night, and she had been right. The "next time" had been better. A lot better. So had the time after that.

Rory stirred against him slightly. He gently stroked the top of her head and she seemed to settle without waking. Then she moved her leg a little higher and a certain part of him stirred in response. He'd suspect she was awake and doing this on purpose, but her eyelids hadn't fluttered and her breathing had stayed shallow. He was tempted to wake her, but he knew she was tired.

He'd have to leave soon, definitely before Miranda woke and preferably before his mother got up. Miranda was too young to understand what was going on—at least, he sure hoped she was—but it was too soon for her to know that he and Rory were together. If this didn't work out, she would be devastated. He had to put her needs ahead of what he wanted, and it would be better to let her get used to the idea slowly.

His mother might very well have figured out that he didn't come home last night, but he still didn't want to get caught sneaking in. Not that he had to sneak. He was an adult, he had nothing to feel guilty about and, a little to his surprise, he didn't. But as crazy about Rory as his mother was, he wasn't ready for this to be out in the open.

For all he knew, neither was Rory. Although, come to think of it, she hadn't minded that her friends were now in the know. From the bed he could make out the outline of the bride's bouquet where she had dropped it on the coffee table. The bride and the other bridesmaids had blatantly conspired to make sure she caught it. Jess had practically tackled two young girls in order to make it happen. Actually, that had been pretty funny.

Not far from the table, the blue gown lay in a heap on the floor along with most of his clothing. Her bra and the twice-removed panties had landed closer to the bed, still within arm's reach, along with the shoes and the box of condoms. More than once during the night, he'd been damned glad the Murphy bed was above his room and not someone else's.

Rory rolled onto her back and stretched, then she opened both eyes and squinted at him. "Are you awake?"

"I am. I was just thinking I should get home—"

"Before Miranda wakes up," she said. "Good idea."

Reluctant as he was to leave, he was grateful for her understanding. He wanted to conduct another intimate investigation of the body that was once again curled against his, but that would seriously delay his departure.

She playfully pulled the sheet off him. "Go. I'll see you later."

"Would you like to spend some time with me and Miranda this afternoon?"

"Love to. Know what else I'd like?"

He kissed her forehead before he got up. "What?"

"Come back tonight and I'll show you."

She could count on it.

Chapter Twelve

Rory staggered up the stairs to her apartment, her school bag dangling from one shoulder and a grocery-stuffed canvas tote bag in each hand. After everything that had happened between her and Mitch in the past two days, she should be feeling totally freaked out. Instead, she couldn't remember ever feeling this domestic, not to mention exhilarated and just the teensiest bit in love. Okay, a lot in love. The past two days had been amazing—the wedding, spending the night with Mitch, going to the schoolyard yesterday afternoon and playing hopscotch with him and Miranda, and spending part of last night with him. He was at work today so she wouldn't see him until sometime tomorrow, and that felt like forever.

She dumped the groceries on the table and let the book bag slide off her shoulder next to them. "I should have made two trips," she said to Buick, who gazed up at her from the chair, sleepy-eyed, as she burst through the door. "Or I could train you to haul your own food up the stairs."

He lowered his head back onto the cushion and draped a paw over his face.

"Right. Like that's going to happen." She changed into a pair of jeans and an old sweatshirt, and was putting groceries away when her cell phone rang.

"Rory, it's Betsy. Is there any chance you can keep an eye on Miranda for the rest of the afternoon? I just got a call from the community center. The instructor who teaches their pottery classes is sick and they've asked me to fill in, and Mitch won't be home till tomorrow morning."

Rory knew exactly when he'd be home. "When do you have to leave?"

"Right away. Do you mind?"

"Not at all. I'll be right down." She hung up, tucked her cell into the pocket of her jeans and dashed down the stairs.

Miranda was sprawled on the middle of the living-room carpet. Rory's chest tightened. As crazy as it seemed, she was as much in love with this little girl as she was with her father. Crazier still, the idea of being someone's mom didn't terrify her. It felt…right.

"Miss Sunshine! Me and Grams were going to have a game of checkers. Will you play with me?"

"That sounds like fun, but it's been a long time since I've played checkers. I might be kind of rusty."

"That's okay. My dad taught me how to play and I'm really good at it, so I can teach you."

Rory settled herself on the floor on the opposite side of the board.

Betsy breezed in from the kitchen. "Thank you so much, Rory. You're a lifesaver."

"No problem. I'm always happy to help."

Rory hadn't seen Betsy since they were at the church on Saturday, and she didn't know if Mitch had said something to his mother or if she had figured it out on her own, but from her expression it seemed pretty clear that she was onto them.

"Can you do one more favor for me?" Betsy asked. "I'm firing a load of pottery and my new kiln is still a bit finicky.

I've already set the kitchen timer to remind myself to check on it. When it rings, would you run down to my studio in the basement and make sure it shuts off?"

"Oh, sure, but I don't know anything about kilns. Can you show me what I need to look for?"

"Of course. Come on downstairs."

"Be right back, Miranda," Rory said over her shoulder. She followed Betsy into the kitchen and down a narrow flight of stairs that led to the basement, which mainly consisted of the low-ceilinged garage.

"My studio is back here," Betsy said.

Rory followed her into a long, narrow room that had floor-to-ceiling shelves along one wall, a workbench along the other, and a potter's wheel at the far end. The lower shelves were crammed with boxes of clay and bottles of glaze, and the upper shelves contained Betsy's latest creations. The air was warm and tinged with the earthy scent of damp clay. The kiln, which was much bigger than Rory had expected, loomed in the corner by the entrance.

Betsy pointed to the dials and switches on the front of the machine. "It doesn't always shut off and cool down when it's supposed to. Someone's coming to look at it again on Monday."

Rory thought it would have made sense to fire the pottery *after* the kiln had been repaired, but Betsy obviously had a lot of experience with this type of equipment.

"When it shuts down, this red light will go off. If it's still on, just turn the dial counterclockwise to shut it off manually."

"That's it?" Rory asked.

"That's it. It's a lot like an oven."

After Betsy left, Rory and Miranda played two games of checkers. Miranda won the first hands down, but Rory narrowly squeaked out a win in the second game.

"What would you like to do now?" she asked.

"We could go to the park."

Rory looked at her watch. "I have to stay here and keep an eye on your grandmother's kiln." The timer was set to go off in about an hour.

"Okay. We could have a snack," Miranda suggested hopefully. "We have ice cream."

Ice cream! "I bought some this afternoon and I forgot to put it in the freezer after your grandmother called. Come on upstairs while I put it away, and then we'll come back downstairs and have something to eat."

Miranda ran up the stairs ahead of her. "Can I play with Buick?"

"You bet. He's probably catnapping, but he won't mind if you wake him up."

The little girl giggled as she hopped up the last few steps and opened the door to the apartment. "Grams has a catnap every afternoon. She says catnaps are better than people naps."

One look at Buick was proof of that. He had moved to the sofa and was sprawled on his back, belly exposed.

Miranda knelt on the floor next to him. "He looks funny when he sleeps upside down."

The cat tilted his head and his eyes opened into narrow slits.

"Hey, Buick," she crooned. "It's me, Miranda."

The cat stretched and relaxed again.

Rory put her half-melted ice cream in the freezer and took everything else out of the bag. "He likes to have his tummy rubbed." The cat didn't have a tendency to scratch and it was great to see young children who were that gentle with animals, but she kept an eye on them as she put everything away.

"Miss Sunshine?"

"Mm-hm?" She really had to talk to Mitch about letting Miranda call her Rory, at least when they weren't at school.

"Remember you promised I could try on one of your bridesmaid dresses?"

Rory checked her watch again. There was still plenty of time before the timer went off. "Would you like to try on one right now?"

"Yes!" In an instant, Miranda was on her feet and standing in front of the closet. "I want the pink one."

Rory hung the empty canvas bag on the doorknob and walked through her living room to the closet. "You like the pink one best?"

"I l-o-o-o-ve pink. It's my favorite color."

"I thought yellow was your favorite color."

"Nope. That was my mom's favorite."

"I see." Rory thought back to the shopping trip with Mitch and Miranda, and all the yellow stuff they'd bought for the little girl. The child hadn't once suggested she'd like something pink.

"I still like yellow a lot," Miranda said. "'Cause it reminds me of my mom."

That was very sweet, and Rory made a silent pledge to honor that while also letting Miranda know that it was all right to indulge in her own tastes. She opened her closet and slipped the cocktail-length pink chiffon dress off its hanger and over Miranda's head. The cap sleeves looked like miniature wings atop the little girl's slender arms.

Miranda stood in front of the full-length mirror, eyes wide and filled with awe. "It's beautiful." She sounded a little breathless. "When I'm a bridesmaid, I want a dress like this."

"Pink suits you," Rory said.

"You wear the green one, 'kay?"

"I wasn't planning to—"

"Please?" Miranda pleaded. "That way we can both be princesses, just like Cinderella. Or bridesmaids."

An idea that held a lot more interest for Miranda than it did for Rory. "Okay."

"Yay!" Miranda admired herself in the mirror on the closet door.

"I have a pink sash in here somewhere." Rory dug through a basket of scarves, belts and other odds and ends. "Here it is."

She had Miranda hold the waistline in place, then she wrapped the sash around her and tied it into a big bow at the back.

"How's that?" she asked.

Miranda twisted one way, then the other, admiring her reflection some more. "I love it," she said. "Now it's your turn."

Rory pulled off her sweatshirt and shimmied into the green satin dress she'd worn at Paige's wedding leaving her jeans on underneath.

Miranda held up the hem of the pink dress and attempted a spin. "Don't you love twirly dresses?"

"You look like a music-box dancer." Rory lifted the lid of an old jewelry box she'd had since childhood, and the little ballerina rotated to the tinny sound of the "Dance of the Sugar Plum Fairy" from the *Nutcracker*.

Miranda twirled again, giggling this time. "I'm a princess ballerina!" She stopped and looked at Rory. "Make your dress twirl."

Rory spun around and laughed along with Miranda. It felt good! Grown-ups needed to twirl more often.

Still giggling, Miranda had another turn. "My dress sounds swooshier than yours."

Rory tried it again. "This dress has a crinoline that's

very swooshy." She took it off the hanger and pulled it on under her dress and over the jeans. She twirled again.

Miranda listened, then spun around. "Mine's still the swooshiest."

"You're right."

They took turns spinning until they collapsed in a dizzy, giggling heap of satin and chiffon.

"That was fun!"

"It was!" Rory leaned against the wall and closed her eyes, waiting for the vertigo to subside.

"Let's do it again!"

They staggered to their feet, hand in hand. "I need to wait till the room stops spinning," Rory said.

Miranda demonstrated her dizziness with an exaggerated swoon. "Oops! Look what happened. My loose tooth!" She held the tooth in the palm of her hand and ran her tongue through the gap in her mouth.

"Better give it to me." Rory grabbed a couple of tissues from a box, scrunched one into a ball, and handed it to Miranda. "Here. Hold this against your gum until the bleeding stops." Then she wrapped the tiny tooth in another tissue, hiked up the dress and tucked it into the pocket of her jeans.

"This means the tooth fairy's coming."

Remember to give the tooth to Mitch, Rory thought. *Or Betsy.*

The cat woke from his slumbers and jumped off the sofa. He seemed unusually alert as he brushed himself against Rory's dress. She picked him up and was giving him a hug when a piercing noise filled the air.

What on earth?

Buick tried to wriggle out of Rory's arms, but she held on to him.

Was that noise coming from inside the house?

Miranda covered her ears with both hands. "Smoke detector," she said.

Smoke? Oh, dear God. The kiln. According to her watch, the timer in Betsy's kitchen wouldn't go off for another fifteen minutes. Rory opened the door to stairway. A strong odor of smoke wafted into the room. She slammed the door.

Should they try to make it down two flights of stairs? What if the stairwell was already blocked? Better to go out on the balcony, she decided. She stuffed the protesting cat into his carrier and grabbed her cell phone. "Come on," she said to Miranda. "I'll call 911 and we'll wait out here for the fire department." She flipped the phone open and forced her shaking fingers to punch in the right numbers.

Once outside, she set the carrier down and grabbed Miranda's hand. "Everything's going to be fine," she said, hoping she sounded more reassuring than she felt.

An emergency operator came on the line.

"There's a smoke alarm going off in my house," Rory said. "And I can smell smoke in the stairwell." She should have soaked a towel in the bathroom and shoved it against the bottom of the door. Wasn't that supposed to stop the smoke from getting in the room?

The woman asked for the address and Rory gave it to her. "The fire department is on the way. Have you left the house?"

"Yes. Well, no. Not really. We're in the attic on the third floor. There's smoke in the stairwell and I didn't know if it was safe to go down, so we came out onto the balcony." She stood with her back pressed against the wall and willed the dizziness to stop before it became nausea.

"How many people are with you?"

"Just one. A little girl that I'm looking after. And my cat." An extremely annoyed cat who associated the carrier with a trip to the vet, and whose plaintive meows had escalated into indignant yowls.

"Any injuries?"

"No. We're all okay."

Miranda looked surprisingly calm. She crouched next to the carrier in a cloud of pink chiffon and tried to stroke the cat's fur through the wire door. "It's okay, Buick. My daddy's a firefighter. He'll rescue us."

Oh, no. What if Mitch was one of the firefighters who showed up? How could she explain this?

"Where is the balcony?" the operator asked.

"Um, it's off the kitchen."

"Does it overlook the street?"

"No. It's at the back." Rory listened while the woman relayed that information to someone.

"Is there a fire escape?"

"No." No way down. Not unless they jumped. She glanced over the railing and the remnants of her lunch roiled in her stomach. *Do* not *look down,* she warned herself. The fire department would be here soon. She hated heights, hated feeling helpless, and hated that she desperately wanted to be rescued by Mitch as much as she agonized over what he would say about this. But facing him was preferable to hanging off the side of a building with only a flimsy bit of wrought-iron railing and fifty feet of nothing between her and the ground below. She'd give almost anything to hear the sound of an approaching siren, but all she could hear were the shrieking smoke alarms inside the house.

"Do you know where the fire started?"

The operator's voice jolted her back to reality. She was still holding the cell phone to her ear. "I'm not sure, but maybe in the basement. My landlady has a kiln down there."

"I'm sorry. What does she have?"

"A kiln. It's a pottery studio."

"Oh, I see. Can you see flames coming from any part of the house?"

Looking for flames meant looking over the edge.

You can do this. The smell of fear actually stabbed her nostrils. No, that was smoke. She sneaked a peek over the edge of the balcony. Real smoke! It was pouring out from the basement window and the garage door that led to the backyard. The house really was on fire, and the smoke was coming from the basement. It had to be the kiln, which meant this was her fault. Had she lost track of time, missed the timer, and forgotten to check the kiln? As she turned the phone to double-check the time on the display, it slipped out of her hand and she watched it fall, as if in slow motion. She was unable to react. The phone hit the balcony floor, bounced once and skittered toward the edge.

Miranda grabbed it before it disappeared. With an outstretched arm, she held it up to her and Rory reached for it with a hand that was shaking so badly, she almost dropped it again. She tightened her grip on the phone. It was their only lifeline, and she had almost lost it.

Miranda looked up at her expectantly. "Are you okay?"

"I'm fine." She wasn't, though. Even her voice sounded shaky.

"We'll be all right. My dad will come."

The operator's voice was buzzing through the phone. Rory held it up to her ear. "Sorry, I dropped the phone."

"That's okay," the woman said, still sounding every bit the voice of reason. "Can you tell me what you're seeing?"

"No flames, but there's smoke coming through the downstairs windows, and there was definitely smoke in the stairwell."

"I need you to stay calm," the operator said in a buttery-smooth voice that was obviously intended to be reassuring. "You've done everything you can. The first truck should be there in a minute or two."

And not a minute or two too soon.

"How's the child doing?"

She was still focused on the cat, kneeling next to Buick in a pink cloud as though she didn't have a care in the world. "She's fine. We're both fine." Except for being in these ridiculous dresses.

"Good. I'll stay on the line with you till the fire department arrives."

"Thank you."

Miranda jumped to her feet, bumping into Rory and knocking her against the railing.

Rory grabbed her hand. "Sweetie, please be careful!"

"Listen!" she shouted. "A fire truck. Can you hear it?"

Rory's knees sagged. Miranda was right. The siren came to a stop in front of the house.

Two firefighters emerged from the walkway between their house and the one next door. One of them was Mitch. He shouted an instruction to someone, but his watchful gaze stayed on them. Rory realized she wasn't afraid to look down, even from this height, because he was there.

"Daddy!" Miranda waved vigorously.

"Hang on, princess! I'm coming up for you."

His take-charge tone was reassuring, and she knew that as soon as they made sure the stairwell was safe, he'd get them out of here.

Several more firefighters appeared, carrying a ladder.

No. No way could she climb down a ladder. Not from this height.

"Miss Sunshine?" Mitch's daughter was gazing up at her, concern suddenly written all over her face.

"Yes?"

"You're hurting my hand."

"Sorry." She loosened her grip on the slim little fingers, but kept a determined grip on the handrail.

"It won't be that scary."

"What do you mean?"

"Going down the ladder. The day you moved in you told Grams you were scared of high places."

Rory had been fantasizing about being a wife and mother, and now she was being comforted by the very child she had imagined herself parenting.

Miranda gave her hand a gentle squeeze. "You'll be okay."

Rory squeezed back and tried to concentrate on breathing. In. Out. In. Out. Shallow, even breaths. If Miranda could do this, so could she.

The firefighters were extending the ladder.

In. Out. Slowly. Hyperventilating now would not be good.

Mitch and another firefighter were both looking up at the balcony. From the sound of things, another fire truck had pulled up out front, engine roaring and siren screaming. All the smoke alarms in the house were blaring. Buick was still yowling and Rory wanted to scream. *I cannot climb down a ladder.*

Maybe they should have gone down the stairs instead of coming out here. Better yet, if they had stayed downstairs, they could have made it out the front door. But then poor old Buick would have been trapped upstairs. She'd heard of heroic measures to rescue an animal, but what if they didn't get to him in time?

The ladder jolted against the balcony railing and the entire platform shook.

Miranda leaned over the railing. "Here comes my dad!"

The ladder shook and bobbed slightly with every step he took. Rory's stomach rolled itself into a tight little ball.

Mitch's worried face appeared.

"Daddy! I knew you'd get us."

He reached over the railing and hoisted his daughter into his arms. Each movement reverberated through the balcony floor and traveled up Rory's body.

"Buick's scared," Miranda said to her father. "So's Miss Sunshine."

His cryptic expression concealed whatever he was thinking about them being out here in bridesmaid dresses. "Give me the cat," he said.

She passed the carrier to him and waited for his next instruction. "Is my mother in the house?"

Rory shook her head.

Mitch relayed that information into the radio clipped to his shoulder.

"I'll wait here while you climb over the railing."

Rory shook her head.

"You okay?" Mitch asked.

She shook her head again, closed her eyes and concentrated on not throwing up.

"She's scared of heights," Miranda said.

"Stay calm," Mitch said. "I'll be right back." He clipped the handle of the cat carrier to his belt and disappeared with Miranda and Buick, leaving her up there alone.

He didn't come back, though. Another firefighter, someone closer to her father's age, appeared a moment later. "We need to get you down from here."

She nodded but otherwise couldn't bring herself to move.

"I'll need you climb over the railing. Nothing to worry about. I'll be holding on to you the whole time."

She gathered up the dress, crammed her phone into her

pocket, and tried to swing one leg over the railing. This was not going to work.

"Can you take the dress off?"

"No!" She was not disrobing up here and climbing down a ladder wearing nothing but a bra and a pair of blue jeans.

"Then turn one of those plant pots over and stand on that."

She did what he asked.

His voice was calm and soothing, and he didn't stop talking even when she was over the railing and had both hands and feet on the ladder. "Once you get the feel of how far apart the rungs are, you can close you eyes if you like. I'm right behind you, and you're going to be okay."

She silently talked herself through every step and when she finally reached the bottom, she had never been so grateful to feel solid ground beneath her feet. Now she just had to face Mitch.

Chapter Thirteen

The firefighter who had helped Rory down the ladder directed her to the front of the house and she quickly complied. Mitch stood there and Miranda was still in his arms. The cat carrier sat on the sidewalk and Buick was still vocalizing his indignance.

"What the hell happened?" Mitch asked.

"I don't know."

"Did you leave something on the stove?"

"No. Of course not."

Miranda wriggled in her father's arms. "Put me down, Daddy. Buick is scared. He needs me."

He slowly set her on the ground, but Rory could tell he was reluctant to let her go. She promptly knelt beside the carrier, the hem of the pink dress puddling around her on the ground. Rory hoped she wouldn't trip on it.

"Your mother went to teach a class at the community center and she asked if I'd stay with Miranda. We went upstairs to my apartment for a while, then we heard a smoke alarm downstairs. I could smell smoke in the stairwell, so we went out on the balcony."

Mitch was shaking his head. "I've asked her not to take advantage of you."

"She isn't! I love spending time with Miranda." She

glanced down at the little girl, who was trying to soothe the irate cat by petting him through the wire door.

"I'll bet the kiln started the fire," Miranda said.

Mitch's eyes narrowed. He gripped her arm and led her a few steps away so Miranda couldn't hear them. "Why does she think that?" he asked.

Rory had been working up to that, but the child beat her to the punch. "Your mother had pots firing in the kiln. Before she left, she set her kitchen timer to remind me to run downstairs and make sure it shut off."

"So what were you doing in your apartment? And what's with this…" He gestured at her dress. "This ridiculous getup."

"We went up to my apartment so I could put my groceries away." She wanted to tell him she was planning to make dinner for him tomorrow, but this was not the time.

"And you forgot to check on the kiln."

"I didn't!" How could he even think that?

"Instead of putting your things away and going back downstairs, you decided to play dress-up."

"Your mother set the timer for five o'clock." Rory tapped the face of her wristwatch. "I didn't forget about it. It's *still* not quite five. I was keeping an eye on the time and we were going to go back downstairs before the timer went off."

He obviously didn't believe her. "You should have stayed downstairs in the first place."

Excuse me? She could understand his concern for his daughter's safety, but his anger with her was totally unjustified, especially since she and Miranda were okay. It was as if he was looking for an excuse to blame her for more than the fire. And now she was just as angry as he was. "This was *not* my fault. The fire started somewhere in *your* part of the house, not mine. I got Miranda and Buick outside,

I called the fire department, and as you can see, we're all fine."

Another firefighter approached them. "Looks like it started in the basement, Mitch. You're sure there's no one else in the house?" he asked Rory.

"I'm sure."

Mitch told him he needed to stay here and keep an eye on his daughter, and he said it in a way that implied he couldn't trust Rory to do it. The other man briefly filled him in on their plan of attack, then disappeared down the walkway.

Mitch glanced over at the cat carrier and a worried look instantly replaced his angry one. "Where's Miranda?"

"Right over—" No, she wasn't. The carrier was open, and the child and the cat were gone.

"She must have let Buick out and chased after him when he ran away. I'm sure they haven't gone far."

Mitch sprang into concerned-parent mode. "My daughter's disappeared!" he shouted to one of his colleagues. "I'm going to look for her."

"I'll look, too," Rory said. "We should split up, though." She lifted the green skirt and dug her keys out of the pocket of her jeans. "I'll take my van."

"Go!" Mitch said. "I'll get one of the police officers to go with me."

Rory hadn't noticed the police cruisers, but now that he pointed them out, she could see that several of them had blocked the street to keep the gawkers at bay. She left him talking to the police, grabbed the cat carrier and rushed to where she'd parked on the street. Luckily, none of the fire engines and other emergency vehicles had blocked her in. She started the engine, released the hand brake, let out the clutch and lurched away from the curb.

Where to look first? Knowing Buick, he would take the path of least resistance, and that was downhill.

She coasted to the end of the block, stopped and looked both ways. No sign of Miranda. One block farther, she stopped at the Panhandle. She clicked on the right-turn signal and glanced left to check for traffic. Miranda, unmistakable in the pink dress, stood under a tree.

Rory swung left, slammed on the brakes to avoid missing a honking car, then sped the wrong way on the one-way street toward the child. Miranda gave her a frantic wave.

She climbed out of the van. "What are you doing here? Your dad and I were worried sick!"

"I'm sorry, Rory. Buick was crying 'cause he was so scared. I opened his cage so I could pet him, but he ran away. I followed him but I couldn't catch him and then he climbed up this tree and now he won't come down."

Sure enough, Buick was perched on a branch, one of the lower ones but still out of reach. She flipped her cell phone open. Who to call? "Do you know your dad's cell phone number?"

She punched in the numbers as Miranda recited them. After several rings, her call went to voice mail.

"Mitch, I found her! We're down at the park, along Oak Street, and Buick is stuck in a tree. As soon as I get him down, I'll bring them home."

Now what? She walked around the tree, looking for a branch that was low enough for her to climb. No such luck. Poor Buick. He was completely stubborn when he got scared like this. He wasn't up that high, though, and he'd ended up on a branch that extended over the sidewalk. She looked around for something to climb on.

"I have an idea," she said to Miranda.

FROM THE FRONT PASSENGER seat of the police cruiser, Mitch scanned the front yards and cross streets they passed.

They *had* to find her. He couldn't let himself consider the alternative. How could Miranda have disappeared without him seeing her leave? If he hadn't been so caught up in arguing with Rory, he would have been watching her. That sounded as if he was trying to blame Rory, and that was unfair, but he needed to blame someone. His mother's house was on fire, his daughter was missing, and until a few minutes ago he'd been thinking that he was falling in love with the woman who was responsible for this crazy situation. All the fear he'd struggled to suppress since losing Laura now threatened to overwhelm him.

His cell phone buzzed inside his pocket, letting him know he had a message. He pulled it out, recognized Rory's number and listened to the message.

"They're on Oak Street, down by the park." Relief surged through him.

The police officer flipped on the lights and they sped down the hill. The cruiser turned the corner, and there they were.

"What the…?" The young officer stopped himself before he said the very thing Mitch was thinking.

Rory had pulled her van up on the sidewalk under a tree. Miranda stood on the grass next to the van, and Rory had climbed onto its roof and was reaching into the tree.

Buick. Mitch had forgotten the cat was missing, too.

They pulled up next to the van and left the lights flashing. Mitch leaped out, rushed around the cruiser and swept his daughter into his arms. "You should have told us you were going after the cat. Rory and I would have helped you look for him."

"You were mad and I knew I shouldn't have opened his cage and I thought I could catch him but he kept running and running."

"I wasn't mad at you, princess."

"You were mad at Rory."

Rory. The zany woman in the green bridesmaid dress was still standing on the roof of her van, trying to coax her cat out of the tree. The cat was just out of reach.

He put Miranda down and led her over to the police car. "Stay in here and *don't* move." Then he went around to the side of the van and tried to get Rory's attention.

She was having nothing to do with him.

"Would you come down and let me get him for you?"

She glared down at him. "I can manage." She had streaks of black mascara under her eyes. Had she been crying?

"He's spooked. I can probably reach him if you let me climb up there."

Rory relented, although he could tell it was grudgingly. She ignored the hand he held out to her and slid off the roof without his assistance.

He would get her to come around, but this wasn't the time or place. He vaulted himself on the van, hoping his weight didn't make a dent in the roof. Rory had already set the carrier on the roof and now all he had to do was wrestle the cat into it. A pair of glittery green eyes offered up a challenge. *Think again, you grumpy old cat. I am not in the mood.*

He got a firm grasp on the freaked-out feline, lifted him off the branch, and scooted him into the cage before he had a chance to react. With the door securely latched, he passed the cage down to Rory and leaped to the ground.

She set the cage on the passenger seat, climbed in behind the wheel, and slammed the door. "Thanks."

Probably best not to mention that the dress was hanging out beneath the door. "I'll see you back at the house?"

"Sure."

She drove away, bumping the van off the curb as she left. He'd performed several bizarre rescues in his career, but his daughter, a treed cat and a deranged bridesmaid? This was definitely a first, and he sincerely hoped it would be the last where these three were concerned. He watched her disappear around the corner, then returned to the police car.

On the ride back to the house, he realized he hadn't tried to contact his mother and he didn't know the number of the community center. Maybe he could get Rory to run over there and tell her what had happened. But when they reached the house, the flower-painted van wasn't there. He had no idea where Rory had gone, but she hadn't gone home.

"Would you mind running us over to the community center?" he asked the police officer. "I need to drop off my daughter with my mother."

THE MORNING AFTER the fire, Rory was back on Annie's sofa. Buick was sound asleep by her feet, as unfazed by the fire and their dramatic third-floor rescue as she was rattled by them. And Mitch had rescued him twice.

If Rory had slept at all, it had been badly. She was distressed about the fire and felt sick for not doing a better job of protecting Miranda, but mostly she was devastated by Mitch's anger. In spite of Annie's assurances that he would calm down once he realized this wasn't her fault, she was overwhelmed by the feeling that their relationship was over.

To add insult to injury, a neighbor had filmed the rescue, including her descent in the green bridesmaid's dress, and had sent it to a local television station. Her phone had started ringing soon after it aired.

Jess had caught it on the TV at the bar and had called Nicola, Paige and Maria. They'd all called Rory, as had several of the teachers she worked with. Then the school principal phoned to say he had already arranged a substitute so Rory could take off as much time as she needed. Just as well, since all her clothes were still in her apartment and all she had here were her jeans, the undergarments she'd been wearing, and the stupid green satin dress.

Later that evening, Betsy had called Annie, who relayed the information that other than the smoke that had filled the house, the damage was pretty much restricted to her studio in the basement. They wouldn't know until today when the house would be habitable again, but Rory would be able to retrieve some of her things. Betsy's insurance would pay for the clean-up.

Do you want to live there? Not if Mitch wanted to end things. From the day she'd moved in, she should have listened to her own advice. They lived in the same house, he was the father of one her students and he was still grieving the loss of his wife. She had known that a relationship with him would get complicated, and she had been right. After Annie had gone to bed, Rory had indulged in a good old-fashioned sob fest. Now, between that and lack of sleep, her eyelids felt puffy and gritty.

Her cell phone rang and she grabbed it from under a pile of balled-up tissues on the floor, hoping it wouldn't wake Annie. It was her father.

Her throat tightened and her eyes went watery. "Hi, Dad."

"Your mother called me last night to tell me about the fire. I wanted to make sure you're okay."

His concern reminded her of being a kid who was finding out that her parents were on the road to divorce— again. "It's good to hear your voice, Dad. I'm so glad you called."

"So, are you okay?"

"Yes."

"You sure, sugar? You sound pretty shaky."

She felt more like a tremor on the San Andreas Fault. "I'll be fine."

"Do you know how the fire started?"

"In the basement." She told him how she'd been taking care of Miranda and that Betsy had asked her to check the kiln, and then the floodgates opened and the whole story poured out. She and Mitch had gone to the wedding together, spent the next day with Miranda, she had loved being part of a family. But he blamed her for the fire, and she didn't know how she could possibly face him again. Her perfect life had turned into a complete disaster.

"The poor guy was probably in shock, Rory, especially after having to rescue his daughter from a burning building. He'll come around once he's had a chance to think things through."

"I don't know. Even if he does, I don't think I can deal with this. We only dated for two days and we ended up having a big fight, with him accusing me of things that weren't my fault. Sound familiar?" That last question had been a cheap shot. "Sorry, Dad. I shouldn't be taking this out on you."

"Rory, there's no such thing as a perfect relationship. No matter how much people love each other, they're going to fight from time to time."

She didn't respond.

"So tell me, do you love him?"

She squeezed her eyes shut to stop the tears.

"Rory?"

"I think so."

"Then you owe it to yourself and to him, and to that little girl, to give this a chance."

"You know I hate it when you're right, don't you?"

He laughed. "Trust me. I know a thing or two about how these things work."

"While we're on the subject of doing the right thing, have you talked to Mom?"

This time it was his turn to be at a loss for words.

"Like you said, you owe it to yourself and her to—"

"You've made your point," he said. "I'll talk to her when the time is right."

"Thanks, Dad. I love you."

"I'll talk to you soon, sugar."

She set her phone on the coffee table and picked up Miranda's baby tooth. She'd put it there last night after she undressed and found it in her pocket. She rolled the small, smooth object between her thumb and forefinger, and she knew what she needed to do.

MITCH'S CAR WAS PARKED on the street when she pulled up in front of the house later that morning. She had borrowed a few clothes from Annie, but she really wanted to pick up some of her own things, and she had to talk to Mitch. She climbed the front steps and went inside. The smell of smoke and wet charred wood was overpowering.

Mitch met her in the foyer.

"I heard you drive up," he said.

She took that as a good sign. She took a little pink satin pillow out of her bag and handed it to him.

"What's this?"

"A tooth fairy pillow."

His eyebrows shot up. "A...what?"

His confusion made her smile. "For Miranda. She lost a tooth yesterday when we were in my apartment. It's inside the pillow."

He stared at it for a moment. "Thanks. She's going to love this, but she isn't here right now. We're staying at

Thomas's place till things get sorted out here. She and my mother are there now."

"I'm staying at Annie's."

"I know. My mother told me."

"I'm so sorry she was put in danger. I might have noticed the smoke sooner if we had stayed at your place, and I wish I had taken her down the stairs when the alarm went off instead of going out onto the balcony."

Mitch shook his head. "Don't apologize. You did the right thing, and none of this was your fault."

"Your mother did ask me to check her kiln, to make sure it had shut off. I might have lost track of the time and—"

Mitch wouldn't let her finish. "You didn't, and that's not what started the fire. The kiln wasn't installed properly— the basement has a low ceiling and the kiln was too close to the walls and rafters."

"How long has she had it?"

"She bought it this summer and had it installed just before Miranda and I moved in."

"Poor Betsy. She must feel sick about this."

Mitch gave her a grim smile. "You obviously don't know my mother. She hired someone to install it, and she's furious that he didn't follow regulations. When she tracks him down, I wouldn't want to be in his shoes."

"You're sure it wasn't my fault?"

"You're off the hook," he said. "If anyone needs to shoulder some of the blame, I have to."

"How is this *your* fault?"

"I knew there was a problem with the kiln's automatic shut-off. I should have taken a look at it."

"But you said that's not what caused the fire."

"It didn't, but if I'd checked it, I might have noticed that it hadn't been installed properly."

Typical, she thought. Classic Mitch Donovan thinking.

According to Betsy, he thought his wife's accident was his fault because he'd had to work overtime and she had gone to pick up Miranda instead. "Do you know anything about kiln installation?" she asked.

His eyes narrowed. "No."

"Then how can this be your fault?"

She watched him shift his weight from one foot to the other. "Making sure Miranda has a safe place to live is my responsibility."

"Sometimes accidents just happen and we don't have any control over them."

Mitch looked startled.

"I'm sorry," she said hastily. "I wasn't talking about your…about Miranda's mother."

"I know. But ever since the accident, it's been hard not to be a little overprotective."

She moved closer to him. "A *little?*"

He smiled and put his arms around her. "Okay, a lot. Can you live with that?"

"Are you asking me to?"

"I am."

"Then I accept."

He kissed her then, and she kissed him back, and she knew without a doubt that Mitch and his daughter were exactly what she'd been searching for. A family.

Epilogue

Six months later...

Mitch stood in the school playground, watching Rory and Miranda on the hopscotch court. The heels of Miranda's running shoes lit up every time they hit the pavement. He'd thought the shoes were a bit over the top, but he was no match for those two, and they'd talked him into buying them. They were safer than shoes with wheels in the soles, they'd told him, and he couldn't argue with that.

"Your turn," Miranda said to Rory after she hopped off the court.

Mitch's daughter tugged on his sleeve, one hand cupped beside her mouth, indicating she wanted to whisper something to him.

He leaned down to her level.

"When are we going to ask her?"

He quickly glanced at Rory, but she didn't seem to have heard. There were still times when he couldn't believe how lucky he was to have found someone who loved his daughter as much as she loved him. Since they'd moved back into the house after the fire, the boundaries between upstairs and downstairs had become blurred and he was ready to do away with them altogether.

Today she was wearing a flouncy canary-yellow skirt and a heavy midnight-blue sweater. She'd used a yellow, white and blue scarf to tie her hair into a ponytail, and her huge yellow-and-blue paisley bag sat beside the hopscotch court. He was always intrigued by her sense of style, today especially, and as he watched her, he knew he was completely and totally in love.

"Ssshhh," he whispered back to his daughter. "We don't want to spoil the surprise." But he was just as excited as she was, and nervous as hell. Scared witless was more like it.

Miranda did her best to whisper more quietly. "Okay. But when?"

Maybe letting her in on the plan hadn't been such a good idea. But then he'd never done anything like this before.

"You have to make sure she wins the game. Can you do that?"

"Yup." That satisfied her, for the moment at least, but she couldn't stand still.

"Your turn," Rory said.

Miranda tossed a quarter onto the court and jumped in.

Rory casually linked her arm with his, and he found himself wishing he could kiss her. And he could, of course. Miranda had caught them several times and she didn't seem to mind, but kissing Rory right now would remind his daughter why they were here.

Miranda wobbled on one foot and faked a fall. "Oh, no! You win." She picked up the quarter they'd been using for a marker and put it in her pocket. "Dad, where's Rory's prize?"

"Right here in my pocket."

Miranda stood beside him and when he winked at her, they both got down on one knee.

For a few seconds, Rory looked baffled. Then she grinned.

Mitch took the jeweler's box out of his pocket. "Rory... Sonora Sunshine Pennington-Borland," he said, fighting back a smile.

"Will you marry us?" he and Miranda said in unison.

He opened the box and she stared at the ring. The few seconds that ticked by while they waited for her answer felt like forever.

"Yes, I will. Of course I will!"

He slipped the ring on Rory's finger, and then she flung herself into his arms, laughing and wiping away tears, and dragging Miranda into their embrace.

"I love you," he said.

"Me, too," Miranda said. "Do you like the ring? I helped pick it out."

Rory held out her hand and looked at it. "It's the most beautiful ring in the world."

"Where are we going on a honeymoon?"

"Rory wants to visit one of the national parks this summer, remember?"

But Rory was shaking her head. "I think we should go to Disneyland."

Miranda squealed with delight. "For real? Are you serious?"

"Totally serious."

With Rory's help, Mitch had come to realize that he was a good father and she was a good mother. Together, they'd be great parents. But that didn't mean they had to be parents while they were on their honeymoon. "You and I can go someplace alone if you'd like."

"A family honeymoon sounds perfect. I can't imagine it any other way."

* * * * *

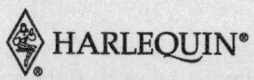

HARLEQUIN®

COMING NEXT MONTH

Available August 10, 2010

A Romance

FOR EVERY MOOD™

Spotlight on

— Heart & Home —

Heartwarming romances
where love can happen
right when you least expect it.

See the next page to enjoy a sneak peek
from Harlequin® American Romance®,
a Heart and Home series.

Five hunky Texas single fathers—five stories from Cathy Gillen Thacker's LONE STAR DADS *miniseries. Here's an excerpt from the latest, THE MOMMY PROPOSAL from Harlequin American Romance.*

"I hear you work miracles," Nate Hutchinson drawled. Brooke Mitchell had just stepped into his lavishly appointed office in downtown Fort Worth, Texas.

"Sometimes, I do." Brooke smiled and took the sexy financier's hand in hers, shook it briefly.

"Good." Nate looked her straight in the eye. "Because I'm in need of a home makeover—fast. The son of an old friend is coming to live with me."

She was still tingling from the feel of his warm palm. "Temporarily or permanently?"

"If all goes according to plan, I'll adopt Landry by summer's end."

Brooke had heard the founder of Nate Hutchinson Financial Services was eligible, wealthy and generous to a fault. She hadn't known he was in the market for a family, but she supposed she shouldn't be surprised. But Brooke had figured a man as successful and handsome as Nate would want one the old-fashioned way. *Not that this was any of her business...*

"So what's the child like?" she asked crisply, trying not to think how the marine-blue of Nate's dress shirt deepened the hue of his eyes.

"I don't know." Nate took a seat behind his massive antique mahogany desk. He relaxed against the smooth leather of the chair. "I've never met him."

"Yet you've invited this kid to live with you permanently?"

"It's complicated. But I'm sure it's going to be fine."

Obviously Nate Hutchinson knew as little about teenage

boys as he did about decorating. But that wasn't her problem. Finding a way to do the assignment without getting the least bit emotionally involved was.

Find out how a young boy brings Nate and Brooke together in THE MOMMY PROPOSAL, coming August 2010 from Harlequin American Romance.

REQUEST YOUR FREE BOOKS!
2 FREE NOVELS PLUS 2 FREE GIFTS!

HARLEQUIN®

American ★ Romance®

Love, Home & Happiness!

YES! Please send me 2 FREE Harlequin® American Romance® novels and my 2 FREE gifts (gifts are worth about $10). After receiving them, if I don't wish to receive any more books, I can return the shipping statement marked "cancel." If I don't cancel, I will receive 4 brand-new novels every month and be billed just $4.24 per book in the U.S. or $4.99 per book in Canada. That's a saving of at least 15% off the cover price! It's quite a bargain! Shipping and handling is just 50¢ per book.* I understand that accepting the 2 free books and gifts places me under no obligation to buy anything. I can always return a shipment and cancel at any time. Even if I never buy another book from Harlequin, the two free books and gifts are mine to keep forever.

154/354 HDN E5LG

Name	(PLEASE PRINT)
Address	Apt. #
City	State/Prov.	Zip/Postal Code

Signature (if under 18, a parent or guardian must sign)

Mail to the Harlequin Reader Service:
IN U.S.A.: P.O. Box 1867, Buffalo, NY 14240-1867
IN CANADA: P.O. Box 609, Fort Erie, Ontario L2A 5X3

Not valid for current subscribers to Harlequin® American Romance® books.

Want to try two free books from another line?
Call 1-800-873-8635 or visit www.morefreebooks.com.

* Terms and prices subject to change without notice. Prices do not include applicable taxes. N.Y. residents add applicable sales tax. Canadian residents will be charged applicable provincial taxes and GST. Offer not valid in Quebec. This offer is limited to one order per household. All orders subject to approval. Credit or debit balances in a customer's account(s) may be offset by any other outstanding balance owed by or to the customer. Please allow 4 to 6 weeks for delivery. Offer available while quantities last.

Your Privacy: Harlequin is committed to protecting your privacy. Our Privacy Policy is available online at www.eHarlequin.com or upon request from the Reader Service. From time to time we make our lists of customers available to reputable third parties who may have a product or service of interest to you. If you would prefer we not share your name and address, please check here. ☐

Help us get it right—We strive for accurate, respectful and relevant communications. To clarify or modify your communication preferences, visit us at www.ReaderService.com/consumerschoice.

HAR10R